# Grandma's Bedside Book

# Grandma's Bedside Book

# Short Stories

# By

# Gladys E. Shaw

Date of Publication: November 2003
Reprinted: May 2004


Published by:
Gladys E. Shaw




© Copyright
Gladys E. Shaw




Printed by:
ProPrint
Riverside Cottage
Great North Road
Stibbington
Peterborough PE8 6LR




ISBN: 0-9546241-0-6

To Elsie and Margaret, my sisters, and to my sister-in-law, Iris, and other elderly folk.

Thanks to Marjorie, Jane and Jo for their help with the typing.

## Author's Note

**Short stories with happy endings, written by the elderly for the elderly, to while away the weary hours of the night when sleep eludes one!**

## Previous Books

**"We came to a village."**
**"I lived in a Village".**

# CONTENTS

*Owing to the nature of her work, Gladys knew, personally, many old people who struggled on 10/= (ten shillings = 50p) per week, and the themes of the Indian stories are based on fact, though fictitious in content.*

# LOVE ME LOVE MY MOTHER!
## or
## An Idyll from an Indian Village

Seven-year-old Kowsalya Pathare looked up, terrified, into a pair of brown eyes that held her own and reflected her fears! 'He was still holding on but at any moment the flood waters could sweep them both away.' How long could he maintain that grip? She could not swim!

Twelve-year-old Ramdas Patil looked down into Kowsalya's terrified face, gritted his teeth and, with one arm crooked round a sturdy babul sapling and one under Kowsalya's armpit, determined to hold on. If only he could pull her nearer the bank, but he could only just hold on and already felt that his arm would be dragged from the socket.

It was at this point that Kowsalya fell in love with him.

\* \* \* \* \* \* \* \*

Kowsalya was a tomboy and tomboys are rare in village India! 'Look at her' her mother would complain, 'she has dumped the baby again and is off playing with the boys!' And the neighbours would see baby Raju sitting in the dust of the village street trickling it through his tiny fingers whilst Kowsalya enjoyed a grand game of 'Hu-tu-tu'. Mother would say, sighing, 'Never will we find a good husband for such a naughty little tomboy.'

Each year Kowsalya's mother took her and the baby on holiday, at the time of the 'Snake Festival', to her own mother's village. This comes in the rainy season so Kowsalya always saw Gevrai at its greenest and best. Then the men folk, using the iron chains that belonged to their ploughs, would put up swings in the old neem tree and the girls and women would swing to their heart's content for two whole days. They would stay with their grandmother for two whole weeks before returning to their own house and fields at Pimplegaon.

The inevitable had happened. Heavy rain had stopped an hour earlier and now the river was rushing by in full spate as the water swept down from the hills. 'Pani ale', someone had called, and the boys and Kowsalya, dragging Raju, had gone down to the bank to witness the sight. The water, churning like milky coffee on the boil, swept past carrying palm trees in its wake.

The boys found bits of wood and threw them into the swiftly moving stream and watched them out of sight. Kowsalya had dumped Raju at a safe distance, saying as usual, 'Now don't you move,' and went off and found two match boxes. She threw one, but the wind caught it and brought it back almost to the bank. Going to retrieve it, she stepped into the water but missed her footing and, before she realised what was happening, found herself swept along by the fast moving stream.

Ramdas, twenty yards further down, saw it happen and, hanging onto a tree, stepped into the water and by some miracle managed to catch her under her armpit, as she swept past! And he held her, but that was all he could do.

Raju was naughty too! He could not see Kowsalya and, bored, got up and toddled home. His two words, 'Kowshi' and 'Pani' were enough to send a frantic mother to the river bank where she saw a passing shepherd run to the rescue of a boy and a little girl and, before she reached them, her little tomboy was actually weeping with relief at being on terra firma again.

In her own relief, she whipped the child soundly as she hustled her home. Stripping off her wet clothes the slaps continued, but later, wrapped snugly in a rough warm blanket, Kowsalya felt only her body tingling and a new glow in her heart as she thought of those strong young arms, that determined face and those beautiful brown eyes that had looked down into hers.

Kowsalya was not allowed to swing or dance at the home of the cobra but when the festival meal was prepared, she donned her new dress, and with a brass dish containing sugar balls, rice and chapattis her mother sent her to Ramdas' home to say 'Thank you.'

Her hero was sitting cross-legged on the floor, pen in hand, doing his homework. Kowsalya, giving him the shy smile of a toothless seven-year-old, said, 'My mother thanks you very much and sends you this food.' Ramdas looked up and saw only the replica of a little city cousin of theirs. His grandmother said, 'You should be ashamed of yourself, playing with the boys!'

That year she counted the days and months to her next holiday in Gevrai, and on arrival, was soon visiting Ramdas' mother. Her big teeth were now well through and she was growing into a very pretty little girl. Grandmother from her corner said, 'What brings that tomboy here?'

The years slipped past with Kowsalya adoring Ramdas from afar. He had left school and, now clad in shirt and dhoti, worked with his father in their fields. Kowsalya, too, had grown up. Now, at thirteen, she wore ankle length print skirts, had two fine long plaits and two large brown eyes that gazed adoringly on Ramdas, (though she would look down shyly when he passed, as girls in India are thought precocious if they look at the boys). If only he could choose to marry her, but again, in India, marriages are always arranged. A good dowry might have helped, but father had already married two daughters. Nothing for it! She must be very helpful to his mother!

Ramdas' mother had just had her fifth baby and had had three sons before having a daughter, who was only just five years old. On the pretext of seeing the new baby, Kowsalya called and stopped to sweep the floor and clean the pots and pans. She took the grain to the little village mill for grinding and helped with the water carrying from the well. Though she made herself busy daily, grandmother, who felt it was her prerogative to run the house, would grumble and mutter under her breath, 'Now what's that tomboy doing?' And Kowsalya would be seen to blush, had her cheeks not been of a soft creamy brown.

Kowsalya, at thirteen, was still eighteen months off marriageable age. Ramdas was eighteen and the oldest son, and all grandparents in India wish to see their sons' sons up to the fourth generation.

Kowsalya sat with Ramdas' mother very often during her holiday that year. One night, when they were sifting grain together, the men came in from the fields, Ramdas, his father and uncle and two men from the city. The visitors had been admiring the land, wells and orchard owned by the Patils. They were still discussing it as they entered the house (the country men slipping off their sandals, whilst the city men struggled with their shoelaces).

'Who are your guests, Mowshi?' asked Kowsalya.

They have come to discuss Ramdas' marriage,' his mother confided to her helper, who visited her neighbours so regularly. Kowsalya's heart missed a beat and she looked hard at the grain she was cleaning as, fighting hard to hold back her tears, her six-year-old dream came crashing around her.

'I do not like it,' went on his mother, but the girl is a relative of grannie there, and it is <u>her</u> wish, so there it is.'

'When will the wedding be?' asked Kowsalya, trying to keep her voice steady.

'In the hot season I expect,' came the answer, but we shall consult the astrologer for the date.'

Kowsalya went slowly back to her own grandmother's house. Lying on a mat in the darkest corner of the darkest room she wept bitterly. Ramdas' mother watched her as she left, thinking, 'That is the girl I would have liked for Ramdas as she understands my ways. Pity grandmother does not like her!' At the end of the holiday Kowsalya returned to her own village.

Feeling there was no consolation in the whole world, on the sixth day after the next full moon, taking an offering on a clean brass tray and water in a brass loti, Kowsalya slipped out of the house and went to the shrine of the Goddess of Wealth. As she poured the water over the red-leaded stone, a passer-by might have heard her murmur: 'O Lakshimi-divi, I have never wanted riches or even a reasonable dowry, only did I want enough to become the wife of Ramdas. O Lakshimi-divi, is it too late?'

The year passed and the rainy season came again. Kowsalya, now fourteen and dressed in saris, refused to go to Gevrai at the time of the Festival and, when is seemed she must go, she took fever so nobody went – deliberately? She could not bear the thought of that modern young city miss who may have captured the heart of Ramdas, or perhaps she did not even like him. Her father would pinch her cheek and say, 'It's time we found a husband for you, but you have lost your sunshine, child. Perk up, or where will I find a husband for you?' And she would answer, 'Perhaps I do not wish to marry.'

They heard in Pimplegaon that Ramdas' grandmother had died and then, in the winter, they received a 'chit' to say that their own grandmother was ill. 'Now we will go,' said Mother, 'and you will come too as you are too big to be left unchaperoned.'

They set out early the next day on the ten-mile walk to Gevrai and never had Kowsalya found the way so long. Her feet and heart grew heavier with every step. Eventually, as the little flat mud houses between the neem trees came into sight, a young man came up the lane towards them. He looked up to acknowledge the visitors as Kowsalya looked up, and their eyes held each other's for a brief second. Kowsalya immediately dropped her gaze. Ramdas felt strangely warm as if he had come home. Those soft, brown, troubled adoring eyes seemed so familiar. Who was the young lady in the pretty sari?

As he went thinking, suddenly into his vision swam a desperate little face from a swirling river and he realised that Kowsalya had grown up. How lovely she was. Ramdas had never thought about whom he would like to marry, but now he knew that Kowsalya was the only girl he would ever want.

Kowsalya arrived tired and despondent. Bathed and fed, she sat with her grandmother for an hour. Gradually, curiosity got the better of her. She must see Ramdas' wife, so went to condole over their bereavement. She was surprised to find mother sitting alone over the evening chores, so asked if her daughter-in-law had gone home for a holiday.

'Daughter-in-law? Then you cannot have heard,' replied his mother. Grandmother died just ten days before the wedding, so it had to be postponed. We suggested Diwali, but her parents would not listen and said they would explore the second offer the girl had had and perhaps she would be happier in the city.'

Kowsalya began to hope again. How glad she was that she had come and that old Grannie who hated her had gone!! Perhaps they would think favourably of her.

His mother's voice broke into her meditations, asking, 'How old are you Kowshi?' I will be fifteen at Shimga,' she replied, then, looking down added, 'and father says I must be married next hot season, but I do not know where he will give me for he says he has nothing for a dowry since he married my elder sisters.'

Kowsalya doubled her efforts to please, but when her own grandmother recovered they had to return home.

Ramdas sat by his mother's side as she cooked. 'Mother,' he said, 'How hard you must work until I marry! A pity my wedding fell through.' 'Yes,' she replied, 'it has been good having our cousin's daughter here these last two weeks. She is such a help, I really do miss her.'

'Mother, supposing Kowsalya was here always, would you like that?' 'I would indeed,' Mother replied. 'She understands what I like, so what does the size of her dowry matter? We have enough of our own.' Father added: 'We must have a village girl. I do not like dealing with city men.'

Three months later, three men arrived in Pimplegaon. Kowsalya's own uncle, with Ramdas' father and uncle. Kowsalya gave them water to wash their feet and to drink. Raju was dispatched to the fields to fetch father home, whilst mother spread a mat on the veranda for the visitors, and then returned to her cooking.

Oh tomboy Kowsalya, have you really mended your ways? She disappeared into the room backing onto the veranda, which had a window. Just a square hole in the mud wall and rather high up. Balancing three tin boxes one on top of the other, she scrambled up to watch the proceedings. Now it seemed that father could meet the cost of a wedding, and she prayed from her vantage point, 'O Bapa, Bapa, please say Yes!' Then one of the visitors said, 'One thing of importance remains, at which Kowsalya's heart missed a beat, as well as her foothold giving way, and she fell with a mighty crash. She was up in a second and through the back door, but was not quite quick enough for her father, who saw her disappearing. Following after her, he caught her arm, swung her round and, boxing her ears soundly, said: 'When will you learn to behave like a lady?' He then returned to the visitors, commenting that the cat had knocked over a couple of boxes. Then Ramdas' uncle finished his sentence: 'It only remains to consult the stars for the date of the wedding.'

Food was prepared and Kowsalya waited on the visitors and the men of the house. Afterwards, she was dressed in a new sari, a present from the visitors and she sat on the floor in front of them, demurely pulling the veil over her face. Silver bangles were slipped onto her wrists as a token of her official betrothal to Ramdas, whilst tears of relief trickled down her cheeks and her heart sang for joy.

The visitors left next morning, leaving Kowsalya counting the days to their next visit, which would be her wedding day.

\* \* \* \* \* \* \* \*

# WHO WAS JOHN WATERS?

The sun was shining again as Jack and Peter cycled the three miles home from school. With only two and a half days to the end of term, what little homework they had had was polished off in prep time. As they crossed the river bridge they dismounted to see how high the water had risen following the dreadful storm that had broken the humid heat of the last few days. On the wide sandy side nearest the town, the long strips of water, now separated from the main stream, indicated how far it had now receded after the flood. On their village side it was just showing the riverbed at the foot of the rocky cliff that had formed over the years where the river swept round the bend when in spate.

They were latch-key youngsters, so having reached the village half an hour later, they dumped their bikes and satchels at Jack's house, swallowed a glass of orange juice apiece, and went down to the river bank to see what might have been left by the receding water. They took Jack's detonator with them. They scrambled down the cliff by the well known path and started making their way over the wet rocks by the water's edge when, to their horrified gaze, they saw first just a pair of legs. They scrambled nearer and found they belonged to a man, clad only in his underpants, with a dreadful gash on his forehead that continued up into his brown hair, to which green weeds from the water were still clinging. Both boys were keen boy scouts and, although only thirteen, knew enough of first aid to know they must act quickly. They turned him over on the flat rock and pressed hard on his ribs hoping to bring up any water from his lungs, and then started artificial respiration to help his breathing.

Then Peter said, 'Jack, I'll stay here doing this and you run home and call the police.' He was away like the wind. Scaled the cliff, raced across the two fields and then, as luck would have it, as he reached the road (well away from the village) he met a man using a mobile phone. They called the police, who called the paramedics from the town.

The police arrived first and whilst one waited for the ambulance Jack took the other to where Peter was wrestling between life and death with the man they had found on the rocks. The police took over; the ambulance arrived following the police car tracks across the fields. They produced oxygen and before long they were carrying the patient up the short cliff path and away to the hospital in the town.

The police, praising the boys for their prompt action, took their names and addresses, and promising them they would hear from them in due course, told them they could go home. However, nothing would induce them to leave whilst the search went on for clues to the man's identity and where he might have left his belongings. Even a tramp would have put his clothes somewhere. How far upstream had he been when he entered the water? How long had he been in the water? It could not have been long after he had hit the rock or he might have drowned. Perhaps he had only just then hit the rock and knocked himself out. After an hour they gave up the search, believing that by then their patient would have recovered sufficiently to tell them all they needed to know.

Peter and Jack, full of their adventure, were taken home in the police car to parents, who by then were beginning to get somewhat worried when the boys had not turned up for their six o'clock tea, bikes and satchels having proved that they had come home from school safely.

Meanwhile, the paramedics had safely delivered their patient to Woodbury General Hospital, the nasty deep head wound dealt with, X-rays taken, he was now safely ensconced in the Intensive Care Unit, to be cared for by Sister Eleanor Jacobs. A policeman remained on duty to get his particulars when he came to his senses.

Eleanor preferred the evening shift to any other as it fitted in with her home life. Her mother, although only in her sixties had Alzheimer's disease that had now taken serious hold on her. She would give her her tea, put her to bed and then the elderly lady next door would come in to sit by her as Eleanor left for the hospital. She would sometimes give her a milk drink and then doze on a folding bed until Eleanor's return at 2 am. By putting the furniture, as was possible, against the walls, they had turned the dining room into a bedroom for her. It was a pleasant sunny room with a French window leading into the garden, where it was pleasant to sit on a summer evening whilst watching over her. Mother rarely sat out now.

Meanwhile, the police and Eleanor watched over their patient, who breathed fitfully, but remained unconscious.

It was the second night at around ten o'clock that he opened his eyes, moved, turned his head, winced and closed his eyes again. Eleanor gently spoke to him. Would he like a drink? He nodded. She produced Ovaltine. He drank a little, pulled a face and then did finish the glass. She called in the policeman, who asked him for his name and address, but he just looked blankly at them. Was he on a journey? He did not know. They agreed to try again the next morning.

By the fourth day he was quite happy to talk. The X-ray had shown no brain damage, but where he could say that he would prefer casserole for his lunch he had not the foggiest idea of who he was, where he had come from, or why he was in the water, and how he had hurt his head. They came to the conclusion that his personal effects with his clothes must have been washed away downstream. It was odd that nothing had shown up after the flood had subsided. They called him John Waters, as he had been found in the river.

Eleanor cared for him from 8 pm to 2 am for five days of every week, and then went home to sleep until 8 am, when she cared for her mother until she went on duty again. She sometimes worked for seven or eight days in succession in order to accumulate a few consecutive days' leave.

John Waters improved daily and in due course was able to leave intensive care to be nursed in a general ward, and Eleanor would look in to see how he progressed before going on duty each evening. Physically, he was better, but she did so want him to recover his memory.

The wound was healing beautifully, but the accident seemed to have caused him to forget everything that had happened to him before the day he was rescued from the river. He did not know his name, where his parents were, if he had any, if he was married with children, or where he lived and worked. All that had happened previously was a closed book. He had never heard of the town called 'Woodbury', before waking up in his hospital bed.

In due course, John Waters was recovered enough to leave hospital, and, indeed, as beds were short he had to leave, but where was he to go? He had no name, no money and address to go to and what would he live on? Eleanor came to his rescue on hearing of his difficulties, and suggested that there was a post going as a hospital porter, and if he would not mind such a humble occupation it would at least give him something to jingle in his pocket, and she added, 'If you would not mind giving an eye to my mother sometimes there is no reason why you should not use our spare room.' 'If I am not around', she added, 'you could always get your main meal in the canteen here, as I do sometimes.'

The hospital found him a pair of jeans and two t-shirts, and Eleanor lent him £20, which he spent in the nearest Charity Shop, purchasing a light jacket, a pair of shoes and undies enough to last him until he received his first pay packet.

John Waters relaxed in this wonderful new environment. Just to sit in a pretty garden outside the French windows in the evening sunshine made 'keeping an eye on mother' a very pleasurable existence. He felt he had never been so happy! Or should it rain, an easy chair in her room watching 'telly' was almost as pleasurable. He was also looking forward to Friday, because Eleanor was due for five nights' leave, and they would be able to share these lovely summer evenings.

They had shared a sandwich supper and were watching television when Eleanor said, 'Do you mind just switching to BBC1. I want to watch the lottery draw. I always buy just one ticket.' They changed channels and while she watched the balls fall John said, 'Lottery! Lottery!' And Eleanor said, 'Oh good, I have just won £10. That will buy me my next ten tickets. John, aren't you pleased?' she added. He looked vaguely at her, murmuring, 'Lottery! Lottery! Winning ticket! Tom Paling!' Then suddenly he almost shouted, 'Where's my bike? It's in the saddle bag!'

'John, what are you talking about?' said Eleanor, worried in case after all their careful nursing his brain was going. 'You said lottery, and it started coming back to me.' 'Yes', said Eleanor, 'Three of my numbers came up so I can collect ten pounds from the post office on Monday.' 'Yes' he said, 'it was that that brought it all back to me. I am not John, but Tom Paling, and one Saturday night all my numbers came up, and rather than put the ticket in the post, and as I was due for my holiday, and always spend my holidays cycling, I decided I would cycle to the head office and collect it in person. Then it had been so hot and humid that day of the storm, and the river looked so delightfully cool as I cycled over a bridge somewhere, that I decided I would take a dip before proceeding, and you know the rest!'

'Oh Eleanor! What happened to my bike? The ticket was in the saddlebag! Oh Eleanor, I am Tom Paling, and for the first time in my life I had money! I was rich for a week and now I have lost it all! You said the police did not find my bike, but surely someone else has by now. I hid it in a crevice in the rocks above the water line, and it must have been found by someone by now. I wonder who cashed my ticket? It was for just more than £TWO MILLION!! I could have been comfortable and without worry. I could have had my own house or flat.'

'Tom,' said Eleanor (it sounded odd to be calling him Tom) 'All is not lost yet and we must have a plan. I will call my neighbour and she will sit with mother for an hour or so, and then I'll phone the police in Stapleton, whom I'm sure will be able to contact the boys who found you, and I'll get the car out and we will go and join them. There is still nearly two hours of daylight so we can begin our search tonight.'

The police at Stapleton were delighted to have a case cleared up, and when Tom and Eleanor arrived a little group awaited them, the boys, Jack's father, and two policemen. It only took a few minutes to cover the half-mile down the road and to bump across the fields to the cliff path. Jack and Peter were soon pointing to the spot where they had found Tom, and the search for the bike began in earnest. Tom thought about six or seven feet from the top, and he had covered it with furze, which might be dead by now. Five adults and two boys spread out over the rocks would be lucky if the bike had not been found by another before them.

They say, 'he who hides can find', and sure enough, after half an hour's search, it was Tom himself who suddenly recognised the spot, removed the dead furze, and sure enough, with all his belongings intact tucked away behind great boulders, was his bike. It was last April, just before Easter, and after two months without memory, he had found it again! It seemed to have sunk further into its hiding place, and took the strength of three men to release it, but release it they did.

Tom at once took the bundle of clothes from his saddlebag, unrolled them, to find his wallet and the winning lottery ticket still intact. He stood stock, still gazing at it, hardly able to believe it was true, and tears coming to his eyes. Practical Eleanor, summing up the situation, put the ticket safely into her handbag, asked the boys for their addresses, promising them that they would hear from Tom shortly, and they all returned to the police station, where Tom left his cycle, and then continued with Eleanor in the car to Woodbury.

\* \* \* \* \* \* \* \*

After mother was settled for the night Tom and Eleanor sat together in the sitting room, drinking a cup of coffee. 'Tom,' she said, 'you really must tell me about your real home, how you were earning your living and who must be frantic for news of you. Is it so far away that our local police have not been able to trace them?' 'Actually,' he answered, 'There isn't anyone to trace. My parents died in a road accident when I was five and I was looked after by a great aunt until I was sixteen. I did play around with school friends sometimes but was never allowed to take them home, so lost them. When I was sixteen my aunt thought she had done her duty by me and put me to an apprenticeship in a metal factory, and I was given bed and breakfast in a hostel. I used to pocket a piece of toast to eat in the evening. The second year was easier because I had 50p above my expenses, but I hated the work I was doing so took myself off to evening classes.'

'There I continued with Maths, which I loved, and studied Economics, and at the end of the summer got myself a job in a bank, and there I still work. They should have wondered what had happened to me and will certainly have to have a certificate from the hospital if I say I want my job back or a transfer to another branch.'

'I was up near Inverness, and in miserable lodgings, and was due for my annual holiday, so when I won the lottery I decided not to risk losing it in the post but to cycle down to the head office with it, and no-one thought it strange as I usually went on cycling holidays. I told no one of my 'win'. I had paid my landlady for the fortnight that I would be away and I have no doubt that when I did not return she put up the 'vacancies' sign in her front window, and that by now another is sleeping in my bed. Coming south I remember coming through Newcastle, so I suppose I am in Yorkshire now. I will have to go and collect my belongings.'

They sat in silence for a little while and presently he said, 'I think I'll give those two lads, perhaps £20,000 each, in trust in a Building Society, for when they are 18, to set them up in life or help them to University, and £50 each for this year's summer holiday, and did you hear what the police told me? A wealthy old gentleman in Woodbury, who has always admired the movement, has given the troop the rest of the money they need for their own Scout's Hut, and it will be named after himself, and bear a plaque in honour of the two boys for their prompt action and efficiency.'

Ten minutes drifted away in companionable silence and then he said, 'I wonder what would be best for us? I am sure you would not want to move mother now, but we could afford full time help so that we could have more time together, and I would apply for a transfer down this way.'

'Tom, did you say 'we' and 'us?' 'Eleanor,' he answered, 'This is the first real, welcoming home that I have ever been in since I was five years old, so if you will have me I'd like to be with you always.' Eleanor slipped into his arms, murmuring, 'And it's so wonderful to feel loved and supported.'

* * * * * * * *

# ON THE RECENT MILLENNIUM

I suppose they thought they had it right,
When dimly lit by lantern light,

A Virgin (Mary) once gave birth
And Lord and Saviour came to earth.

'Twas BC four, but some say seven
When earth received this gift from Heaven.

But theologians are few
So let's pretend they really knew!

About that time the count began
But only if a Christian land!

Then if we turn our history pages
We soon must come to Middle Ages.

We go through Romans, Celts and Angles
That leave the mind in right old tangles.

When Wessex, Sussex each had kings
To deal with their own local things.

Or did the Bishops hold more away
The pope, of course, too far away!

Who came to rule in 999?
'Twas Ethelred, the next in line.

He came and went and came again
When in due course he chose to reign.

The public did not find him steady!
In history he is known 'Unready.'

And did they note a thousandth year
To celebrate with right good cheer?

Perhaps the public as a whole
Preferred the stories that were told!

Canute tried hard to rule the sea
Against the tide! That couldn't be.

That Alfred burnt a batch of buns
'f more interest than millenniums?

But some who felt the end was nigh
Gave cash and jewels they'd had by!

More kings and queens have come and gone.

War and peace! Sports and song!

Until a second thousand years
Has passed, with all its hopes and fears.

So! Build a Dome! Set up a wheel!
Light a Squib and try to feel

As daylight dawns that this is great,
And quite the way to celebrate!

But! Ten's the end! So are we wrong?
Year one should be millennium!

* * * * * * *

# SUMMER STORM

Jenny stared at the blackened evil smelling saucepan just as her husband had walked in! Returning from work, he had strolled into the kitchen, planted an affectionate kiss on the top of her head and said, 'What a clever little wife I have! Can't even make the gravy without burning it!' This was the last straw! Throwing the pan in the sink Jenny screamed, 'I'm sick of the lot of you. I am going out and I don't care if I never come back!' Two seconds later the front door banged and Jenny was gone. Bill, lost for words, stood gazing at the closed door and then realised that his eight-month-old daughter was crying.

The day was still sunny, very hot and humid as Jenny ran from the house and down the road. It did not matter where, she only wanted to get away from it all. Perspiration was running down her face and her blue cotton t-shirt clung to her back leaving great damp patches! It had been one of those days and she just could not take any more.

The unusual heat had lasted more than a week, and their lovely little daughter was suffering from 'prickly heat', making her irritable and unable to sleep, even in the daytime at her usual times.

She had taken three-year-old Timothy to play school, and for the first time he had refused to settle without her, and had cried so distressingly that she had had to stop and play with him until he had settled. This procedure had upset Rebecca and she cried all the way home.

Arriving home she went to prepare the child's mid-morning drink, only to discover that the milk had not been left, as usual. She had phoned the depot and was told that two rounds-men were on holiday and one had gone off sick, and they would try and get it to her in the afternoon or she could pick it up from the depot. Forget the baby's drink and her own coffee, but get into the car and go down to the depot. Pick Timothy up from play school, get the children's lunch, wash up, including the breakfast dishes, that were still in the sink, and put the children down to rest. Beds were too hot and they would not settle; perhaps a rug in the garden would be better, and then just when Rebecca had fallen asleep Timothy had wakened her, trying to make her smell the daisies he had picked. Who'd have children!

(She was getting out of breath, and slackened her pace whilst trying to hold her damp shirt away from her sticky body. Heavy clouds were gathering in the west. The air seemed heavier and hotter than ever).

Water! That was the answer! She had pumped up the paddling pool, stripped off the children and popped them in. Timothy could get himself in and out but she dare not let go of Rebecca. It was backbreaking, trying to hold the child upright, but when she put her on the grass she yelled loudly until she was back in the water. Meanwhile Timothy had decided that the flowers needed a little refreshment, and in trying to water the roses from the pool had fallen into a rose bush. Sit the baby on the grass, wash the dirt away, fetch the dettol, get out a persistent thorn, and assure him 'it's all better now.'

At 5 o'clock Jenny took them and prepared them for bed before giving them their tea. Even that had had its problems. Timothy had eaten his scrambled egg and bread and butter, and then upset his orange juice all over the table. By the time she had mopped it up and got him into a clean night-suit, Rebecca refused to take another mouthful.

(Jenny had reached the sea front! Had she really walked a mile? She sat down on a bench on the promenade and breathed in the refreshing ozone).

The bed! Is there anything worse than trying to get two fractious children to bed on a hot night? Well, let them play a little longer whilst she prepared dinner for herself and Bill. Rebecca had fallen asleep on the sitting room floor, so turning the gas down under the vegetables she thankfully swept her upstairs and into her cot. She then took Timothy up, covered him with a sheet and, scattering a few Dinky toys on his bed, said he could play for a little while.

Back downstairs she laid the table, turned the chops and mixed the gravy, added the vegetable water, and had just got it on the gas when a penetrating yell from Timothy caused her to forsake all and rush to his bedside. He had somehow pinched and wedged his finger between the wheels and undercarriage of one of his little cars. She had managed to ease it out and taken him to the bathroom to wash and plaster it, and as she settled him in bed again, she realised that the outcry had disturbed Rebecca, who again had to be quietened. She then returned to the kitchen to find she had left the gravy on the gas, and it was now reduced to a charred mass. Then Bill walked in!

Jenny sat down on the sea front, full of self-pity and self-justification. Nobody, just nobody, had to put up with the difficulties of her life. All Bill had to do was to eat the breakfast that <u>she</u> had prepared, and drive off to the peace of his office, and to return to a good meal ready and waiting for him each evening. Breadwinner indeed!!

There was a blinding flash of lightning, followed immediately by such a loud crack of thunder that Jenny jumped out of her skin, and almost came back to reality. It would serve him right if she did not ever go home again, and then he would realise what her life was like.

Large drops of rain began to fall. It was so refreshing that she threw her head back, and enjoyed it as if she was under the shower. She had done right in walking out! Let <u>him</u> cope with their children for a change! She crossed over to the railing and watched the large raindrops splashing on the swelling rollers. She was wet through and cool. She watched the blue fork lightning splitting the sky as the thunder roared. It was a magnificent sight! Why had she never walked out in a thunderstorm before? How Bill would enjoy it! Bill? What was he doing? Had he had his dinner? Serve him right it if had gone cold! The rain was easing off and the storm less noisy. Jenny began to realise that she was not just delightfully cool, but cold and hungry! The clouds were breaking here and there, and rain lessening and the air cool and fresh.

Jenny came to her senses. What a fool she had been! Had today been any worse than any other day? Were the children crying for her? How was Bill coping? She started to run to the nearest bus stop and then realised she had no money with her. She looked at her watch. She must have been out for an hour, and was a mile from home. Her thoughts were in turmoil. Had Rebecca cried herself into having a fit or something? Now she was running, and the road seemed endless. What was Bill doing at this moment? Never had a mile seemed so long.

At last, Springfield Gardens. She reached the house but had no key and Bill, fear written all over his face, opened the door with a red-cheeked baby in his arms. Seeing Jenny wet and bedraggled on the door-step, he dumped Rebecca on the floor, and gathered her into his arms, murmuring, 'Honestly Jenny, I was only joking!'

The summer storm was over.

* * * * * * *

# COCK-TAILS FOR TWO
## or
## The Peacock's 'Tale'

Arnie rocked sadly to and fro, and although no sound came, the tears flowed steadily down her cheeks. If only there was something she could do! Something that would give her a little hope. A year ago life had seemed full of sunshine, and now she could not bear to think of her future.

Rozann had been a kind husband, and as his fourth wife, she had been much favoured. He had longed for a son, but his first wife having presented him with sickly twin daughters, who died shortly after birth, had remained barren until she, too, died four years later. He could not believe his ill-luck when after three years with his second wife he was still childless, and following the local custom of his Indian neighbours, without turning her out, he took a third, and after another four years, yet a fourth wife.

His forbears, immigrating from the middle east to India, had settled in Mumbei, in the eighteenth century, and the business they had started was now in the third generation, flourishing, and he longed for a son who would carry on in his place. Arnie had been only seventeen at the time, but in the twenty years of her marriage she had borne him eight children. True, only two were boys and only three of the six daughters had survived, but she had made Rozaan very happy indeed.

They had a beautiful home in a village situated in the hills beyond the city, and there was no shortage of money, but of more value than his gifts to her was the love they shared. There would be flowers on the couch they shared at night, and he would feed her Halwa and Jellabies until her sisters-in-law grew so jealous, they constantly chided and teased her when he was not around. But she had Rozaan, who loved and cherished her because she had given him children in his old age.

Now Rozaan was dead! He was nearly seventy and she had always been aware that she was an old man's love, but that did not make it any easier. Her sisters-in-law teased more than ever, and often only served her a meagre portion of food, when she had done most of the cooking. Her great consolation was that in two years time Agzaan, her eldest son, would take over his father's share, and work with his uncle in their very flourishing business in Mumbei, and when she had arranged his marriage the management of the household would be hers. But now even that little hope had been wrenched from her.

A virulent epidemic of smallpox had broken out, first in Mumbei, and had then reached the village. Already twenty-four had died and now, not one, but both her sons had caught the germ. Sixteen-year-old Agzaan was full of spots, and the fever so high she did not think he could survive the night, and the younger boy's temperature was rising hourly.

Her married eldest daughter had arrived to help with the nursing, being equally concerned for her two brothers, who were now getting delirious. They bathed their foreheads with scented water and gave them draughts of cool Nimupani (lemonade) to drink, but nothing helped the situation. They had wealth, and a beautiful home, but money could not buy back two young lives, Arnie thought, as she looked down on the two who might be wrenched from her before the night was out. The future would be bleak indeed, thought Arnie, as, struggling to keep calm, she had gone out into the garden in the cool of the evening, to prepare herself for this last night's vigil.

As she sat silently weeping under the gulmohor tree, a gentle voice asked, 'But why so sad? Would you like to tell me about it?' Surprised, she wiped her eyes and cheeks to find that she had been joined by a Holy Beggar, who was sitting quietly by her side. Arnie found relief in confiding in this stranger, and told her the whole sad story. The old crone listened, nodding wisely, and finally said, 'I will tell you a cure, but you must be very brave;' and in a voice scarcely above a whisper told her what she must do. Could she? A woman? Her family respected by the whole village. Dare she?

It was growing dark when she hurried back inside to consult with her daughter. She tried to freshen the two invalids, and make them more comfortable. She replenished the nimbu-pani, kissed her daughter, draped a large black shawl over her head and shoulders, and went out into the starry night. She was glad there was no moon.

It was no great distance to the Rajah's palace, and as her eyes grew accustomed to the dark, she was able to keep near to the trees so as not to be seen. On arrival, the huge gates were, of course, locked and barred, and she knew that there would be more than one watchman on guard.

As the old woman had said, round to the right was a huge banyan tree, whose long roots hanging from the boughs might help in scaling the six foot wall; and so it proved, and in due course with her heart hammering in her chest she dropped down into the Rajah's gardens. Now to find what she had come for!

In bare feet, walking silently over the well-scythed lawns, straining her eyes to find what she wanted, the inevitable happened! A small group of the Rajah's peacocks were disturbed. Immediately, there was such a great squalling and shrieking from the birds that the dogs began to bark and the guards were aroused, and Arnie, abandoning her search, ran for her life back to the banyan tree. She knew she had a three hundred yard start from the gate and that the dogs would not be unleashed because of the birds, but even so, for a non-gymnast to scale nine feet on the roots to reach a sturdy branch was no mean feat, especially as she could see the bobbing lanterns drawing nearer!

Terrified of falling, she crawled a little way along the branch, and not knowing whether she had passed the perimeter wall or not, she stopped to conceal the creamy skin of arms, legs and face in her flowing dark skirts and shawl. She hardly dared to breathe when the guards stopped and waved their lanterns aloft, and when the dogs sniffed around the hanging roots, then passed on. She waited until they had returned to the gate, murmuring something about nocturnal creatures, before descending, having noted the fact that she was now beyond the wall.

She retrieved her sandals from their hiding place and stood, concealed by the wall, weeping.

The frightened peacocks were now strutting on the walls and Arnie, beneath, leaned against it, weeping with frustration and fear, and knowing she dare not again risk entry, when something soft brushed against her hand! She stooped to find out what it was and discovered it was a peacock's tail feather, complete with its blue-green eye. If there was one, there could be more. She groped along the base of the wall, and sure enough she found a second. Her mission fulfilled! Two beautiful fresh feathers, bearing the round blue-green eye of the peacock. Cock tails for two! Would the Holy Beggar's remedy work?

She almost ran home, soaked them in water scented with jasmine, used it to bathe the foreheads of her invalids, then placed them under their respective pillows and sat down to wait and watch. She was back in time!

Gradually they grew quieter, their ramblings ceased, and slowly, but surely, the high fever abated. First the elder broke out in such a sweat that they had to change his sheets twice, and later the younger one, and finally at about 3 am both boys dropped into a deep and natural sleep, whilst mother and daughter stood by, by now weeping with sheer joy. Peacock-tails for two! Some say that peacocks' feathers bring ill luck, nevertheless the old Holy Beggar's remedy had worked, and the boys would live to see another day.

Morning came, and as Arnie looked out on their beautiful sunny garden, she thanked the Powers that Be, knowing she could, indeed, look forward to a rosy future.

# THE VILLAGE FETE
## or
## 'Fate'

Mrs Maxwell, now wearing her habitual scowl, peered over her garden hedge, and up and down the road, then ducked as the two young girls passed. Then as the click of their high heels died away, up she popped for a second look. 'Disgusting,' she thought, 'Her t-shirt might be neat but those pink shorts were disgusting! And the other! Oh yes! A nice flowing ankle length silk skirt, but she was nearly coming over the top of that bodice! Disgusting! There was no other word! What was the village coming to?'

They were threatening to close the village Post Office, too, and the next thing would be the village shop! Not that she ever used it, as the town, where a greater variety was to be found, was only a 6p bus ride away! A gentle breeze stirred the dust in the lane and she thought, 'When will they tarmac this lane again? We pay our taxes, don't we? Oh yes, the council wants our money but they are not prepared to spend it on amenities.' Oh no! The village wasn't the same since her dear husband had died, aged only fifty-nine, and that was now five years ago.

Why didn't her daughter come to see her now? It couldn't be because she had sent Emily into the house for screaming in the garden, and that she had smacked Daniel for pinching a cherry off the cake! Children had to be disciplined. It was her daughter's duty to come and see her mother, with or without the children. Everything was wrong since her husband's death.

Why do people want to change things? Even the Church? Last week the vicar had actually lighted a candle. Never! Never! Never, had they had candles in their church. She challenged him but he made excuses. He said that just as the electricity had failed it had clouded over and he could not see to read his book. 'Thin end of the wedge,' I said. 'First steps to Rome!' Why is everything getting so bad since I lost my Alfred?'

26

'Look at the village itself. Last year they were trying to 'prettify' it, just to enter the prettiest village in Sussex competition. Well, I didn't hang up messy baskets of flowers to please them, and in any case my front garden is always pleasant to look at! I naturally take a pride in it. And then all that band playing and singing just because they won. I can't think what the other villages must have looked like. Now what do they do for this year but decide on a village fete?!!'

She went indoors but it seemed dark after the garden. She took a deck chair outside but it was cold in the shade and too hot in the sun. In the distance she could hear the band playing at the fete, and she had seen the swing boats and the hand operated roundabouts arriving and wondered what other stupid things they were doing. Taking her old Panama hat she thought she might as well just walk along there and see. She nearly turned back when saw there was an entrance fee of 6p for adults, but having got so far, and at least she was never short of a penny, she paid for the ticket and walked in.

As she walked forward there was the roundabout on her right. Happy children sitting on tigers, elephants, bears and horses, and going up and down and round and round. She felt almost a lilt to her step in time to the scraping, grinding tune, that seemed to come from its inside. Then there was a table game, and further on the under sixes were fishing for little celluloid toys round a paddling pool. How her little grandchildren would have enjoyed this! She could have put Daniel in for the under three section of the beautiful babies' competition. He was far better looking than some of the fubsy faced children lined up there, and much more lively.

A few steps further and someone had set up coconut shying. 'Sheer profit,' she heard herself murmur as ball after ball missed its mark. 'I bet he knew that a lot of mugs would never knock one down.' 'Oh, mugs are we?' said a nice friendly 'village fete' kind of voice, 'I'll bet you your entrance fee that I can do better at it than you!'

What came over her she will never know. She suddenly felt young again! Captain of the school stool-ball team, when she could hit that wicket fair and square, right in the centre, and slash that ball to the boundary! 'Oh!' she heard herself saying, 'Five balls each.'

Her first missed! He said, 'Told you so!' The second target wobbled then fell; third and fourth were clean bowled, and in her excitement the fifth missed. 'Three out of five,' she declared triumphantly! 'Excellent,' he agreed, and then managed to hit one himself.

They, neither of them, wanted coconuts, but he said that at least she deserved a cup of tea as her prize, and lightly putting his hand under her elbow, steered her towards the tea tent. As she went she met the two half clad young girls again; now with escorts, and she smiled at them as they laughed over ice-cream cornets, melting in their hands.

He brought the tea in thick white cups, and fresh cream scones, to their table. They were delicious, and never had tea seemed so refreshing. 'This is kind,' she said, 'and I do not even know your name.' 'Tony Scott,' he answered, 'I have seen you in church, but I am new to the village. I lived in Brighton, and when my wife died three years ago, I decided that when I retired I would buy a cottage in the country, with a bit of land, and grow turnips to compete in village competitions! I have bought 'May Tree Cottage.' I was looking round last year and I thought this was the prettiest village I had ever seen!'

Mrs Maxwell remembering a small tin of salmon, sitting on her larder shelf, found herself suggesting that perhaps he would like to try her elderberry wine and have a bite of supper with her, before returning home. He accepted, and bought her a large bunch of cut flowers, that had just won second prize!

Dear Mrs Maxwell! As she climbed into bed that night she made up her mind to 'phone her daughter and beg her to bring the children over again.' She would explain that she had been out of sorts when they visited last. She would tell her, too, about the fete, and how much she had enjoyed it. If they have another next year she must bring the children over, she would say.

She turned over, and as sleep came she thought, it really did not matter if the vicar lit a dozen candles to read his book!

* * * * * * * *

# TO TELL OR NOT TO TELL?

King Edward died! George took the Crown
When I was born in Bromley town.

So parents and my teachers, too
Were all Victorians through and through.

And in that dark Victorian day
Two subjects were 'taboo' they say.

God was one. Except by priests
Who week by week and Holy Feasts,

For hours on end they warned us all
That hell awaited, should we fall!

And close behind this harmless text,
The never to be mentioned; 'SEX.'

In twenties, thirties, times had changed,
But Mum and Gran had stayed the same.

And as those mid-Victorians feared
A modern era then appeared.

A child saw kittens born one day,
'Is that like us?' she dared to say.

But Grannie hustled her to bed,
'We don't discuss such things,' she said.

'She'd find out how babes were carried,
On the day that she was married!'

But out in India, Oh My!
How could that rigid rule apply?

But May from England; that old school
Thought even here they knew that rule!

A princess, May had eyed with scorn,
Because she knew how babes were born!!

Poor May! How horrified she'd be
Had she heard two schoolboys say to me?

How yet another daughter came,
They had, as yet, to choose her name!

'Yes!' Mother started in the night
But baby came when it was light.'

And now my problem comes to view
When I confronted infants, two.

'Emma says her Mum will try
On shopping day, a babe to buy.

I've sisters two and brothers four
Mum didn't <u>buy</u> them. Eh? Miss Shaw.'

I found myself in real dilemma
Tell the truth, or side with Emma?

But in a flash an answer came;
'A babe is costly, just the same.'

'Just think of all the things you need,
Pram, cot, clothes and baby feed.

It's very dear!' then hurried on.
Before more questions, I was gone!!!

\* \* \* \* \* \* \*

*By way of interest, when I was three and my sister five, we were once taken for a walk and out to lunch by a young girl in the village. When we got home we found the doctor had given Mammy a teeny little new baby because she wasn't very well and would have to stay in bed for a few days!!!!*

*GES*

# NEVER BE A BORROWER OR A LENDER

'Ai! Ai!' screamed Kalika, as blow after heavy blow fell across her thin shoulders, and then as she crumpled under the wicked beating, administered by her husband, 'O God, help me!'

Sumput, seeing his wife in a dead faint on the floor, threw down his stick and stepped outside into the village alleyway. Most of his relatives had assembled by then and were gawking with interest through the open doorway, realising that Kalika was being beaten up, and as he stepped out they tried to push in. With this he thrust them aside, went back for his stick, and, without a word, set out purposefully on the twenty-four mile walk to town. He could reach Gevneer tonight, sleep there, and complete the journey before 8 am in the morning, if he resumed his walk before dawn.

He was not really a bad man, just badly frustrated, and as he walked tried to justify his action! He had told her to get hired for the day, and at least get some grain for the family. She cannot have tried hard enough!! The fact that he had not been hired either, he tried to put to the back of his mind. He was, in fact, angry with himself, as he did know in his heart of hearts that it was through his own pride and stupidity that they were in the plight they were. At all costs he must save their few acres! No! It was because she had not had work for three days that now there was nothing in the house and the children starving. It was her fault. She should have tried harder and brought something home. They were her children as well as his. Oh dear, supposing he had killed her!

It was already agreed that they were to have a twelfth part of one of the head-man's fields, as harvesting wages, whilst he, at the same time, would cut their own with his eleven-year-old son.
Oh, why oh why had he borrowed? And likewise, oh why oh why had he lent? It had just happened! These things do! It was not his fault!

It was two years ago. In the middle of a good harvest, a man from a higher caste than his own, asked to borrow half a sack of

33

grain just for a week or two, he would return it at the end of the 'gathering in.' Sumput had been so flattered to be asked by a man of a higher caste that he agreed at once, and said of course, that for so short a time interest would be waived aside.

But harvest came and went and there was no repayment. Whenever Sumput plucked up courage, and politely requested repayment, he was assured of repayment by the next week, and the borrower would add, 'you've got my IOU haven't you?' But a scrap of paper is not a half sack of grain to families who live from hand to mouth. That was two harvests ago, and last year owing to out of season heavy summer rain, the harvest was so small that Sumput, himself, had had to borrow half a sack, to be repaid this summer, by a whole sack - the recognised rate of interest.

The whole year had been such a struggle, but this year the fields were reasonably good, and Sumput looked forward to being in the clear again and determined never to lend or borrow again. If he could just keep going for the next month or so. She knew their struggles. She should have tried harder. 'God,' he murmured, 'Let me find her alive. I couldn't kill her. She is the mother of my children.'

Back in his village, when Sumput had left, mother-in-law had silently sprinkled water on Kalika's face, rubbed her cold hands and consoled the weeping children. There was no milk or sugar in the house but she boiled water, and from half a teaspoonful of tea dust made a cupful, and supporting her aching back, held it to Kalika's lips.

Sumput arrived late in Gevneer, but a cousin/brother gave him a little bread from their meagre larder, and his wife's mother made him some tea, with neither milk nor sugar. He ate, drank and slept, and before dawn he was on the road again to cover the last ten miles to town before labour would begin.

He found a building site and, despite his hunger, on being hired he kept going all day, and received his daily wage in the evening. At last he could eat, and went to the nearest eating house, but was careful not to spend more than half his earnings, and even from that meal he saved half of the bread and chutney for the morning!

For four and a half days he worked hard and well and was promised work for the next week, and now with two days' wages still intact he bought twenty pounds of millet, and started for home. He was unused to the heavy work of carrying baskets of bricks up homemade ladders, but work he would until the time came for reaping his own millet. He hoped young Devdas was faithfully bird-scaring morning and evening. He was quite good with the sling these days!

As he walked, he thought of Kalika at home. Supposing he had killed her? She was such a good wife he could not think why he had been so stupid. Even frustration should not have made him lose his temper. 'O God,' he prayed, 'please don't let me be so foolish again, if only I can find her and the children safe and well.' He rested for only a couple of hours in Gevneer, in order to be home by nightfall.

Meanwhile, Kalika had not been idle in his absence. On the following morning she had risen with Devdas before sunrise. He had gone off with his sling to their field, and she had wearily picked up her six-month-old baby, tied him to her aching back, tied a bit of rag round her upper arm to keep the flies off where the skin had broken, and taking the axe, set out on a three mile walk to the hills, hoping to gather a load of wood. And find wood she did, which she hawked round the village among the well to do, and was rewarded when one kindly soul gave her a measure of grain in exchange for her load.

The second day with a neighbour, the baby and the axe, she met a friend as they were about to set out, who asked how she did and if she had eaten that day. Kalika, with all the love and loyalty of the good wife that she was, replied, 'Yes, we shared two big breads this morning! My husband, you know, has gone into town to see if he can find work for a week or two, but we had no grain in the house on Monday, so yesterday I went out to see if I could find any wood, one has to go so far these days. But I managed a load, and the headman's wife bought it from me for a measure of grain, sufficient for two breads. I did the grinding and made the bread yesterday evening, but I knew the children would be hungry again this morning, so we saved it until now. So we have had bread today. We are now just waiting for two other women and then we are going to the same place again, hoping to find enough for another load.'

Sumput arrived after dark, and being a warm night, he found the children asleep on the ground outside his home. Kalika, still awake, and gossiping with her neighbours in the moonlight, stopped in mid-sentence with joy and surprise! Whilst he lifted the grain from his head and dumped it on the ground she brought water for him to drink and to wash his feet. Then she hastened inside and blew up the tiny fire to a red glow, put a little musur (red lentils) on to boil, crushed their last two chillies with salt, and added them to the lentils.

In fifteen minutes, with that day's two breads that she had been saving for the morning, she was able to put a meal before him. When it was ready she spread a mat and called him in. Never had simple food tasted so good! He pulled her down beside him and fed her with his fingers, as they had done on their wedding day, and later, as they prepared for sleep, he fed her with 'jellabies' (an Indian sweetmeat), murmuring, 'Have you forgiven me? I promise you I will never do such a thing again. And I have found good labour that will last until we reap our harvest and our debt is paid! God is good!' They fell asleep, at peace with themselves and the world.

\* \* \* \* \* \* \* \*

*The facts of this story are true, but drawn from three 'eye-witness' episodes.*

*GES*

# WIENER APFELSTRUDEL

Betty was introduced to Brian's German Grandmother at their wedding. She had come over especially for the occasion, as Brian was her only grandson. Medium height, but on the big side, hair still showing vestiges of blonde in the two plaits, folded across her head, giving the appearance of a halo to her pleasant, open, hardly wrinkled round face; two clear blue eyes, that seemed to pierce Betty from top to toe, completed the picture. She had returned to Germany before the young couple were back from their honeymoon. Nevertheless, it soon appeared to Betty that Grandma had moved in with them!

'My Grandma's house was absolutely spick and span.'

'You never saw a speck of dust in my Grandma's house.'

'My Grandma's garden was as neat as her house was clean.'

'My Grandma was an excellent housekeeper.'

'My Grandma taught my mother all she knew about cooking, so mother was an excellent cook, as Grandma had always been.

By then, Betty was heartily sick of Grandma! There seemed to be no end to her virtues!!

However, the worst was yet to come. The summer was drifting into autumn. Daily, Betty seemed to be picking up windfalls that fell from their four apple trees. She, too, was a careful housewife, and was making them into pies and other puddings, or just making a puree and putting them into the freezer. Then Grandma popped up again!

'My Grandma makes a delicious Apfelstrudel. I think she made it with noodle pastry or something! (Apple Stroodle! Whatever's that?) I'd love some Apfelstrudel again, especially as it seems such a good year for apples. Grandma used to, sort of, roll it out on a cloth, and then she tipped it, all rolled up, onto a baking tray! It rolled itself up like a Swiss roll, only nothing like a Swiss roll really!!' (Oh dear!)

Betty, though terrified at the thought felt she must have a bash at it if she could find a recipe. She flattered herself that she was a reasonably good cook, as she had had no disasters up to the present, but then casseroles were no great problem!

After a visit to her mother-in-law she carried home a book neatly covered in brown paper and labelled, 'Continental Cooking'. The book was in German. She did find the page for 'Apfelstrudel', but of the recipe only the words apfel, sultanen and kilogramme were recognisable. However, having the correct spelling she now looked again in Mrs Beeton's 'Everyday Cooking', and sure enough 'Apfelstrudel' was there.

One Kg of flour. Good Heavens! That would be enough for an army, and she decided to cut the amounts down to half. Fancy making pastry on a board! She made a well in the heap of flour and poured in the beaten eggs, melted butter and warm water, and prepared to do battle with the spatula. Easier said than done! She tried a wooden spoon as if she was making batter, and finished up prodding, poking and pounding with her hands until she was well over her wrists with the sticky mess. Betty realised too late that she had not cut the liquids down to half and it was all too wet, but by frequently flouring her hands it helped considerably.

Now for the difficult part! Rolling it on to a floured cloth was bad enough as the sticky parts would come through, but trying to stretch it until it was tissue paper thin was a sheer impossibility. It would have to be ¼ inch thick!

On went the sliced apple, the sultanas, breadcrumbs and sugar, and it was ready to roll. Or as near as it ever would be! Gently she lifted the cloth. Nothing happened! She gave it a little shake, but still it remained glued to the cloth. She gingerly lifted it again and gently shook it. Perhaps a little too high or too vigorously? Her Apfelstrudel leapt from the cloth and collapsed in a messy heap on the pastry board. She scooped it up, and putting it into a basin, murmured something about a steamed pudding another day. But now? What? It was 6 pm. If at first you don't succeed . . . CHEAT! She got the car out and rushed down to the supermarket. After all, most things <u>can</u> be bought ready-made!

\* \* \* \* \* \* \* \*

\* \* \* \*

*THE ODD WRINKLE*

*Four-year-old Rosemary sat on Grannie's knee, listening to her bedtime story. As the familiar words unfolded one small dimpled hand caressed Grannie's chin. Suddenly she sat upright and asked: 'Grannie, why doesn't your skin fit your face like mine does?!'*

\* \* \* \*

## OUR ONE BRIGHT STAR    <u>Subject –Starlight</u>

A village church, complete with spire,
Eight men, four boys, made up the choir!

Post Office, Shop and Public Bar;
Scattered cottages, near and far!

A village green with a tadpole pool!
Leafy lanes, a village school.

The pupils numbered thirty then
But Betsy Green made up for ten!

With Betsy life was always fun!
Playing together, in the sun.

Football, Races, Cricket Matches,
Batting hundreds, missing catches,

Follow-my-leader through the copses
(Sometimes getting stung by wapses).

Comic Role or Tragic Queen
In concerts, on the village green.

Betsy shone in class or play
Always clever, always gay!

* * * *

Her family moved in the month of May.
The sun went in: the skies were grey.

No races now or matches won
Our youthful leader – up and gone!!

How dull the village, drear the green.
Birds and flowers, rarely seen.

It always rained – the wind was keen
As we mourned the loss of Betsy Green.

* * * *

As years slipped past the village slept,
We grew, worked, married, traditions kept.

Women's Institute, here and there
Annual Whist Drive, Village Fair!!

A cinema fixed for a winter's night,
To entertain us with delight.

A screen, projector men in action
To guarantee some satisfaction.

The programme promised, 'Fun for all
At sixpence each in the Village Hall.'

The Hero? One named Thomas Brady,
Elizabeth Greenfield, Leading Lady!

Elizabeth Greenfield? There? On screen?
Never! THAT is Betsy Green!!

Laughing, loving Betsy Green,
Our hearts went back to the village scene.

Dear Betsy! Now ascended far!!
Our radiant, own, illustrious STAR!

* * * * * * *

# LONGING FOR HOME

He must not do that again. His body was cool enough – but his head was, oh so hot, under the Mediterranean summer sun that he had nearly fainted or fallen asleep! He must keep awake! He had managed to kick off his hampering trousers and swim into an oily patch of water, but he must keep awake! Supposing help never came? He wondered how long ago it was that the torpedo had struck!! That was at fourteen hours and thirty minutes, then they had lined up for the ropes, say another ten minutes, and he had been the last down at his station. What had happened to the Padre? The ship had listed before he had time to follow, and he had three small children at home. Were they now 'war orphans'? He wished he could see other members of the crew. War was so cruel. How long had he been in the water? The palms of his hands were burned with the friction of the rope, and the salt water made them sting.

What was Marzi doing? Was the sun shining like this in England? Was she resting in the garden, or drinking tea? Perhaps it was time for evening watering? He was glad he had fixed the hosepipe for her. Would he ever laze in the garden again?

Oh the sun, the sun! He tried to turn his back on it or float on his stomach, but, chiefly, he must keep awake and not think of home. How long was it now since he had seen Marzi in the kitchen, or the garden at home? Perhaps he would never see her again! How long had he been in the water? His watch had stopped on impact at 14.45 hours.

Could he see a boat, or was it a hallucination? He tried to wave but his arm was so heavy. He lifted it a second time. Was it a boat? Was it turning and coming nearer, or just his imagination? Surely a boat was coming nearer, and after hours, it seemed strong arms were pulling him aboard. He recognised seven others of his crew already on board.

When he tried to talk, his voice cracked because of dreadful thirst, and the palms of his hands were stinging with pain. On asking the time he found it was nearly seventeen hours, so his ordeal had, in fact, only lasted a couple of hours. But he felt sick and his head was spinning, so he closed his eyes. He thought for a couple of minutes, but when he opened them again he found he was dry, dressed in someone's old army battledress, lying on a bunk and a kind sailor trying to persuade him to drink some clean cold water.

He asked the time and where he was and was told he was on a Destroyer that had been in convoy with the 'Medway', and added admiringly, 'Wonderful precision, you know. Just wonderful, to get that ship right in the centre; the mother ship of all our submarine work! There was no time for your lifeboats. From the torpedo striking to her listing was just twenty minutes, and only ten from the command to 'abandon ship'! It was about seventeen hours when we dragged you from the water and it's now nearly 20 by the clock. You've had a good sleep and I expect you'll be ready for something to eat, soon. Can you hold a spoon with those bandages on your hands? You may have a touch of the sun by the colour of your face, but you'll do now.'

Two shipwrecks in six months. On the 'Southampton' it had been aerial bombardment, and they had only abandoned ship after a day and a half of fighting the fire, and left in orderly fashion. However, the bomb had gone straight through the telegraphy area, killing the three on duty. He, too, was a telegraphist, but they had just changed shifts!

Oh War! War! War! Wrecking the lives of the young and saddening the old. What would Marzi feel if he did not return? And the Padre had a young family and did not come down the rope! What of his family?

What fun it had been growing up. He remembered the car he had bought for five pounds when he was seventeen. Everything he knew about cars he had learned on that old Morris. When it broke down completely he had left it in a ditch somewhere near Henfield and sold its parts for three pounds, to a garage in the vicinity. He remembered the Sunday morning outside Cuckfield Church, when he had been camping nearby with two of his sisters. He had cranked and cranked and when, at last, the engine had sprung to life, the rest of the congregation, standing by their Rolls or Rovers, had clapped and waved as he chugged away. His sisters, and dear Marzi, would he ever see them again?

Day-dreaming between vivid dreams of sea, fire and ropes, he awoke to find they were in the Suez Canal, on their way to Durban. Physically, he felt fine, the dizziness had passed, but he felt sick with apprehension, as he hoped they might be making for England. However, after some days, on their arrival at Durban, he learned that the 'Medway' survivors were down for home leave, but England, now, must be at least two months away. They rounded the Cape, and at Simonstown he, and his colleagues, changed ships and were at last on their way home.

They asked for 'watch' duty, to while away the long days, and were rewarded with a lighted passing ship with a great Red Cross in lights on her deck. A hospital ship.

They made for mid Atlantic first, but after weeks it seemed they turned eastward for home. All that troubled war area as yet to be negotiated. They zigged and zagged, but he felt they were still travelling eastward! Nothing! What would he find if he ever did arrive? If only he knew their present location. As they drew nearer, and the danger increased, he felt more and more remote from reality.

He had gone to his bunk at 4 am, but at 8 am he was awakened by clanging and shouting. Scrambling into his clothes he rushed up on deck and 'lo and behold'! They were arriving! Surely that was Birkenhead to starboard, so they must be heading for Liverpool. He was Home! There was a lump in his throat, and tears not far away, as they chugged up the Mersey to the final phase of his journey home. It was ten before they went ashore, and another couple of hours dealing with customs, and being issued with new clothes, at last Lime Street Station, train to Euston, tube to Victoria. Time. . time. . time, but at last the train for Brighton, at dusk, on a late summer's evening.

9.30 pm and Brighton Station had never seemed so welcoming. All in darkness, but he found Trafalgar Street, as his eyes grew accustomed! St. Peter's Church! The No. 26 bus! He had heard of bombs on Brighton, but all seemed intact and normal, and he was on his bus for Hollingbury.

He had had no news for so long. Perhaps his mother had been bombed out. Perhaps the family had moved. The nearer he got, the more apprehensive he began to feel. Supposing they were not there!! He knocked on the front door of 'Hinton'. It was 10 pm, and all was blacked out. The door opened an inch, and a voice said, 'Who is it? The Warden?' 'No! Does Mrs Shaw live here?' The chain was off. Blow the Warden! The door was opened wide. 'Doug,' said Florence, 'why ever didn't you phone to say you were coming?' He was in the sitting room. He was embracing Marzi. Both with tears running down their faces. The nightmare was over, and home just the same.

\* \* \* \* \* \* \* \*

*Note – As this is a true story, may I add that Doug next put to sea on an Aircraft Carrier that sailed to the Far East, and he did manage to hear from the Padre again, (through one of those small miracles) and learned that when the 'Medway' listed, he was thrown clear on the far side, picked up by another Destroyer, and I think taken to Egypt.*

*GES*

# TROUBLE AT THE EMBASSY

'She's a poker face if ever there was one,' remarked Nelson, as he sat down at his desk and pulled the 'in' tray towards him. He had just come through the new secretary's office and met with the usual curt overture! He was a sociable soul, fancy free, and was used to 'getting on with the girls'. After all, their immediate circle hardly numbered a hundred people, a little European community in a large Indian city, so if you did not get on with your fellows it was, indeed, a sad situation. Nelson loved all, and his openhearted ways endeared him to all, Indian and English alike.

'I think you are right,' answered Bill, 'a poker face indeed, but I feel it is a face only, and perhaps hides a heart that is broken!'

'Broken hearts aren't in my line,' commented Nelson. 'Here we are shoved together in a foreign country for three years, in which to sink or swim, I'm swimming through mine. Hail fellow well met! That's my policy. See as much of the country as you can at the Embassy's expense and,' he added, rather more thoughtfully, 'try and get to know the people as well. I am glad I learned Hindi; it brings you much nearer the heart of a country when you can converse whilst on trains and buses. It was quite an experience attending the wedding of Devchandra's daughter last week, and jolly nice of them to have invited me!'

Bill would have liked to have gone to the wedding too, but he had not had Nelson's easy-going ways, and his Hindi was not quite so fluent, but he was the more sincere character of the two. He sat down at his own desk, thinking of the sad grey/blue eyes of their joint secretary, which shone, almost glistened, from such a straight face. He wondered why such a pretty, pleasable brunette should have such brusque manners. He liked the combination of her light eyes and dark hair. She had been with them for more than a week now and they did not know where she lived in New Delhi, what family she had in England, or even if she had a home there.

On arrival, she had informed that she was 'Miss Perkins', until Nelson had cut in with 'Oh, come off it, we are all on Christian name terms here, at least between ourselves,' and so she had conceded to being called Sarah.

Bill was sure something had gone wrong in Bombay, but did not know what he could do to put it right, even though his chivalrous nature longed to do so. He had only heard that she needed a change and so had been transferred to Delhi. The new girl, who had been on her way out from England, had gone to Bombay (now called 'Mumbei') in her place.

*'It can't be a change of air she needed,'* thought Bill, *'for nothing could be worse that the humidity in Delhi in June, prior to the onset of the monsoon.'* He was thankful for his air-conditioned office and daily dreaded the impact with the outside world that enveloped him like a warm blanket when he stepped onto the pavement at 5 pm each evening.

Bill, too, was a little lonely at times, as Nelson, his colleague, had so much of his time fully booked with outside engagements, but with a book on the roof of the penthouse flat they shared, under the stars, when the evening breezes were a little cooler, he found relaxing. One of the happiest ways of spending one's leisure hours.

They muddled along very happily together in their flat with their one 'cook-come-butler' servant, whom they knew swindled in moderation, but shopped well, cooked excellently, fed them promptly, and never seemed to mind how many visitors they had, even at short notice, or how many hours he worked. Their life seemed to be his life, and the three of them seemed to get on very well together.

In the outer office Sarah got down to the day's letters. *'Type hard, type quickly, type efficiently, think about the job'* went through her mind, as she slipped another piece of paper into the machine. *'Don't let your mind go back, don't think about it – them! No! Just be a good secretary, and never mix work with romance again.'* How thankful she was that England was so far away and that she had been able to write casually, 'we have decided to postpone our wedding, Jim feels he would like a little more time, perhaps later in the year. We feel, too, that it might be a good thing if we did not see quite so much of each other, so I am asking for a transfer to Delhi . . . I will let you know my new address as soon as I am settled there . . .'

Her parents had been surprised, of course, and even suggested that they wait until they were in England again, pointing out that she would still only be twenty-five when her specified three years would be completed. 'But what about the wedding dress?' they had asked, 'would it not rot in that tropical heat?' Soon she must write and say that it was 'off' for good, but she felt she would never be able to write the whole truth. How could she tell them that her beloved Jim was actually married to the girl who had shared her flat in Mumbei, and that they were enjoying their honeymoon in the cool, clean, fresh air at Simla, in the foothills of the Himalayas, whilst she literally stewed in her own juice in the humidity of the pre-monsoon period? How could she tell them that soon her old address would be their address?

How blind she had been! How lightly had she said, on more than one occasion, 'I'm terribly sorry, I might be another hour yet, but do go round to the flat, Ellen will keep you company until I come.' How well had Ellen been keeping him company, even whilst all three had been discussing the preparations for her marriage to Him! She wondered how often his telephone calls had been deliberate when she was working late.

She dragged her mind back to the letter in the typewriter, as she felt her cheeks burn with shame at the recollection of her stupidity and blindness over the months, since Ellen had joined her at the flat.

Bill came in with a tape. *'How pretty she looks when her cheeks are rosy,'* he thought, and then looked away quickly when he saw a tear glistening on her long dark lashes. He hastily retreated to his inner sanctum.

Two weeks before the fateful day, when Jim had taken the bull by the horns and burst her dream bubble forever, was the one and only inkling she had had that things were not quite as they had been before. Their acquaintance was longstanding, as children they had been neighbours, until Jim's family had moved away. Then, after ten years, they had met up in Oxford again when she was a first year, and he a second year, student, and they had drifted into an easy friendship, which had developed into love and culminated with an official engagement. Had it not been Jim himself, who had persuaded her to apply for work at the Embassy, so that they need not be separated during their engagement? How rosy had been her horizon, when she bid her parents goodbye at Heathrow, to board the waiting plane that would take her out to Jim, and an adventure in India.

And then last April – really only two months ago! Years seemed to have lapsed since then! A group from the office had been celebrating a birthday party in the little café at the Hanging Gardens on Malabar Hill. How beautiful Mumbei had looked that night, as they gazed down on the lighted city and admired the 'Queen's Necklace' (the lamps that encircle Back Bay). Her whole personality had been full of love and joy, and yet Jim had scarcely even held her hand when the others seemed to have gone ahead.

*'Type! Type! Type!* She thought, *'Don't think, concentrate on work!'* But the long hot nights were often sleepless and she would live again the awful moment, when, over ice-cold drinks at the flat, the truth had been blurted out.

'You know Sal, I just can't bear hurting you. I mean, I know I was responsible for bringing you out here. I honestly did think we were in love, but now I don't think we were. I just think we sort of got along all right. You know, meeting up again like we did, we just, sort of, drifted into it . . .' and he had waffled on, embarrassed, until Ellen had come down to brass tacks with, 'You see, if he really loves me, your marriage could hardly be a success, could it?'

In a voice and a heart that belonged to someone else, she had agreed that of course it would be stupid, and she quite understood, and they had thanked her for being so 'jolly decent', and the only difference it had made was her transfer to Delhi because she could not bear to see their happiness.

Never again would she dare let love creep into her business world. *'Type! Type! Type!'* and click, click, click went the keys of her neat electric typewriter.

At 5 pm Sarah stood on the street. The heat shimmered on every side. There was a breeze that stirred the leaves of the trees like the blast of a furnace. It would be hot at the flat, but it was hot standing there. Cold drinks only helped for a minute or two, (how many glasses of water had she drunk since lunch?) It was too hot to eat and yet one felt limp with hunger. The only bearable hour seemed to be the hour before dawn. Had it really been this hot on her arrival in India twelve months ago? Perhaps the swimming at Breach Candy, and the gardens at Malabar Hill, had offered a little respite.

She stood at the corner wondering – should she take a rickshaw and just go home? It was too hot to walk, but what was the point of getting there quickly? Why hadn't she swallowed her pride and returned to England at once instead of enduring this awful heat of the summer in the pre-monsoon days (still ten days to go, folk said). The cinema perhaps – they had fans, and they opened all the doors between films, and it would pass the evening away. But it was too hot to be so close to so many people. If only the rains would break. Walk home slowly and kill more time. But even the traffic passing was hot and the constant screeching of brakes, as the rickshaws and taxis wove in and out of each other's paths, got on her nerves. People said it was even worse in Calcutta, she wondered why there were not more accidents. She felt so alone, so desperately alone, and in a foreign city a long, long way from England.

As she stood wondering a gentle hand was laid under her elbow, considerably startling her, but the voice was familiar and as gentle as the touch. 'Hello Sarah, not gone home yet, and you left almost ten minutes ago.' She looked up into the concerned eyes of Bill and was glad it was not Nelson, as he would probably have slapped her on the back and asked her what she was doing mooning on the corner.

'I was waiting for a rickshaw,' she lied, 'but they all seem to be full.'

'Have an ice-cream first, now that we have met up,' he suggested, 'they have Kwality in the Natraj not far from here.'

Sarah hesitated, but the pressure on her elbow increased, indicating the suggested direction, and she fell into step beside him, an unhurried step befitting to a hot evening in the East. Bill had amazed himself with his courage, and could hardly believe that she had acquiesced so easily, and it was with joy that he began to anticipate one evening when he would not be alone reading on the roof.

They slipped through the doors of the air-conditioned restaurant, and the sudden draft of cold air made them shiver as they seated themselves on the cool cane chairs. The place was practically empty as the evening rush had not yet begun, and Bill was so glad of company that he wished his ice cream could last him a couple of hours.

He looked at Sarah and longed to ask questions, and wished again that he had been gifted with Nelson's ready tongue and could ask outright where she hung out and where she spent her evenings and why the sudden transfer from Bombay? As Sarah seemed lost in her own thoughts, once they were ensconced, it made him feel tongue-tied and awkward. *'Why was she so uncommunicative?'* he wondered. At last he managed 'I come here quite often after the office in the summer. It is good to have a place where you can sit quietly in the cool, apart from the ice-cream.'

'Yes, it is good,' said Sarah, 'I did not know there was such cool refreshment so near at hand. You see, I don't know Delhi at all.'

'No, of course you don't,' answered Bill. 'Tell you what, I am on my own quite a bit, as Nelson has been out here longer and has so many friends. Why not let me show you round at the weekend? The Red Fort, and some of the temples, are well worth a visit.'

Sarah froze, what had she done? She had slipped into a situation so easily – she was getting involved. It wouldn't do. Pleasure and business never! It was a fatal mistake. She had been off her guard. Why had she accepted the ice cream? She had not thought of it leading to a date, of course it was only a 'once and then forgotten' date, but would it be like that? She had to meet this man every day in the office. No! No! No! Not at any price must she get involved again. What a fool she had been, why had she not gone straight home as usual? She realised how easy it had been to yield to the gentle voice and commanding masculine touch and for a fleeting moment feel secure again.

He had issued an invitation, and it seemed an eternity before she found her voice and lied, for the second time that evening. 'Thank you very much,' she said, 'you are very kind, but I am afraid I am busy this weekend,' and then hastily added 'and the next, but some other time perhaps.'

Bill's heart sank. An even longer silence followed. He had bungled everything. He had frightened her off, but did not know how or why. Oh well, he had only tried to make her happy, because she seemed so capable of happiness, but always appeared desperately sad. The waiter brought the bill and a little saucer of roasted aniseed. Bill threw a few of them into his mouth whilst waiting for his change, but Sarah ignored them; lost in thought.

Outside once more in the hot street, they smiled at each other and Sarah thanked him for the delicious ice cream, adding unnecessarily that it was 'gorgeous'.

Bill, loath to let her go back to her emptiness and sadness, half-heartedly suggested, 'Why not get changed? I could wait for you and then let's have dinner somewhere,' but he knew the answer before he spoke.

Sarah, for her part, knew he was only trying to be kind, and hurriedly declined, murmuring something about another time and must get home now. He beckoned a rickshaw for her and the next minute she was gone.

Bill walked slowly to Queen's Square, found number sixteen and took the lift up to the penthouse. If only I was better with people, he thought. I was all right at college; I got on well with everyone. It said so on my testimonial. Perhaps here our world is so small there is not an 'everyone' to get on with. He looked over the parapet at the street below. He saw the taxis, the rickshaws, the buses, the tongas and hundreds of office workers in their gleaming white clothes, and girls in pretty saris, all going somewhere. There was certainly no shortage of people, but here he was alone. Was Sarah, too, looking out from a veranda at the passing crowds?

* * * *

The weeks passed into months. The monsoon broke with the usual violent electric storms, and eased off into a pattern of generally heavy rain with intermittent sunshine. July, August and September, and people began to look for the clear blue skies, warm days with cooler nights of an Indian winter. Bill had made no further advances towards Sarah, who was still icily doing their typing in the outer office.

Owing to the cancellation of her wedding and honeymoon, Sarah had had no hot weather holiday and the understanding manager of her affairs in Mumbei had suggested that she have a few weeks off in October. By way of conversation one morning Bill casually asked where she would spend her holiday, mentioning by name some of the hill stations that would be clear of mists by October.

Sarah, without thinking, had answered, 'OH, I expect I will go to Simla; it's cool there and an acquaintance of mine once said it was worth a visit.'

Bill mentally added, *'Yes, and you just keep away as I want to keep myself to myself.'* He did not pursue the subject any further.

Sarah, meanwhile feeling somewhat more cheerful at the thought of a holiday in the Himalayas, found a tourist office and booked in at another hill station in case Bill followed her. She knew he was also due for two weeks leave.

In due course, she was settled in a first class compartment of a train bound for Kathgodam, from whence she would climb up to seven thousand feet in a matter of two hours by bus to a place chosen at random, called Naini Tal, in the Himalayan foothills.

Higher and higher climbed the bus. One hairpin bend after another as they seemed to literally climb the face of the mountain range. At last, topping a seemingly impossible height, Naini Tal (the Lake of the Goddess Nain Naini) was spread before them. It was breathtakingly lovely. It was as if the bus had reached the rim of a gigantic saucer filled with water. Surrounding the lake was a metalled road with houses and hotels, and from there the wooded hills rose to perhaps another seven or eight hundred feet. Other roads between the trees must have existed, as houses here and there were visible between the trees. Here, indeed, she could wander alone. But was that what she really wanted?

She dragged her eyes from the view to the dreadful shouting and pushing, which now surrounded the bus as it came to a standstill.

All were demanding her services, 'Coolie Mis Sahib?' 'Me strong man Mis Sahib,' 'See my number!' 'Dand Mis Sahib?' 'Only one rupee Mis Sahib,' 'Me seven number Mis Sahib!'

Never before had she had to fend for herself in such a shouting mob and she was petrified. An educated young Indian came to her rescue, asking if she required a coolie or a dandy, (a chair to be carried in) and where was her destination? She named the hotel, which proved to be less than three hundred yards away, and very soon her new friend had her suitcase and bedding roll on the head of a coolie, and with instructions to pay him one rupee on arrival he bade her good evening. Twenty minutes later she was ensconced in her hotel bedroom and had ordered her evening meal and breakfast to be sent up to her. She spent her first evening reading all of the 'tourist' information that had been given to her in Delhi, but as she looked out on the hills she wondered if she would dare climb them alone.

She was happy enough for a week visiting the local gift shops and bazaars with a view to buying presents to take home. Carved boxes and ornaments, beautiful hand-painted papier-maché trays, Kashmiri embroideries and brassware – what to choose? She could not make up her mind! If only she had a companion with whom she could explore these wonderful emporiums.

On Friday night it rained, but Saturday dawned clear and bright. At 7.30 am promptly, a knock on the door announced arrival of the bearer with her breakfast tray. He was always very cheerful and chatty, but today particularly so. 'Good morning, Mis Sahib, very _good_ morning today, Mis Sahib. Mis Sahib must go Dorothy's seat.'

'But Shunker-rao,' said Sarah, 'I do not know the way and I cannot climb the hills alone!'

'Yes, but you go Dorothy's Seat _today_ Mis Sahib! Many, many peoples going today. Last night much rain and today sunshine! You go early and you climb and you see far away white, white snow, and you see Naini dive Mis Sahib. Big, big white mountain. Today you will see because last night rain! Not always seeing, but today, yes!'

He went on to tell of the path on the other side of the lake and that there were finger posts and how first she would come to a green plateau called Tiffin Tops, and then taking 'small, small' path and climbing more she would come to Dorothy's seat. He added as he left, 'Many people go to Dorothy's seat today.'

Meals taken alone do not take long to consume, so it was still quite early when Sarah set out to follow Shunker-rao's instructions. A guide would have been help, but there were cairns and she arrived at Tiffin Top without much difficulty, but the 'many, many people' were apparently all later risers. On and up she went, and as the way now was rather rough going she regretted not wearing her walking shoes. She had not imagined it quite so rocky, but eventually the long slow climb was over and the view magnificent. Fold upon fold of hills and there, in the distance, a whole range of gleaming white snow, beautiful against a clear blue sky. Shunker-rao was right; it was indescribably beautiful.

She looked around for somewhere to sit whilst she feasted her eyes on the vista and find her camera. She had thought she was the first on the mountain that morning, but as she rounded the rocks, a few yards away, dressed in casual flannels and tweed jacket, she startled a lone walker, already enjoying the beauty of the morning.

He turned, and neither could believe their eyes, as Sarah murmured, 'Bill' and Bill stammered, 'I, I thought you were in Simla, that's why I came here.'

They stared unbelievingly at one another until Bill, taking a leaf out of Nelson's book, said, 'But we may as well make the best of it, and see, there is room for us both here,' and Sarah, after the long climb in her thin shoes, was glad to be sitting down to rest.

Oh dear, she had not reckoned on how it would feel to be with a young man in a tweed jacket and slacks again. Back her mind went to the quads and cloisters of the Oxford colleges, when she had sailed on top of the world. Was it really only Jim that had made for happiness in those seemingly far off days? Come back to the present. Here she was literally on top of the world with one whom she knew would enjoy her companionship, and with a friend she could be a little more venturesome in these beautiful hills.

Bill thought, *'if only I could help her come out of that shell, if only I knew what the barrier was, if only I had a friend with whom to share this holiday.'*

They sat in silence, and talking trivialities, for perhaps half an hour, and then Bill said, 'I was up here yesterday, Sarah, and about this time a char-walla lighted a fire on Tiffin Tops and was brewing up for climbers. Let's go down there – I could just do with a cuppa.'

Sarah rose gladly, she was more than ready for refreshment, and they started to go down the stiffest part of the path. He was a step or two ahead, and as he paused and looked back to give her a hand over a particularly rough patch she caught the heel of her stupid shoes and took a tumble on the sharp uneven stones. She had ricked her ankle slightly and, grazed and bruised, she burst into tears.

Tears, tears – not really because she was hurt, it was hardly anything, and not because it was undignified to tumble. It was the pent-up emotions of the last six months coursing down her cheeks as he lifted her from the ground and carried her to a nearby rock. Through her tears she tried to assure him that she was not seriously hurt, but he still had his arm around her, and he drew her to himself, and with his own cheek caressing hers whispered in her ear, 'Try Sarah, do try and tell me all about it, and perhaps it won't seem so bad. I, too, am lonely, and have so longed to be friends, what is troubling you? I'm sure it could be mended or forgotten.'

Sarah dried her eyes, and immediately began weeping again as bit by bit the whole unhappy story came out, but as she talked she nestled into the comfort of that strong arm in its college type tweed jacket, and memories of Jim began to recede. Could it have been her pride, not her heart that had been so badly bruised? Had Jim been right? Had they just drifted into it? Oh dear! Dare she risk it all again? Bill was here – she needed him. He said that he needed her too.

She snuggled into his arms, and looked up into his so very caring face; as he looked down to her and gently put his lips on hers. Her holiday began from that moment.

* * * *

Two months later, in a village near Chigwell in Essex, Mrs Perkins picked up the morning post and seeing a blue airmail from India eagerly opened her daughter's letter.

'Dear Mum and Dad,' she read, 'You will be surprised when you read this, but I am sure it will make you as happy as I am <u>now</u>! Our wedding is arranged for March 1$^{st}$, and it is to be held at a lovely little English Church at Naini Tal, in the foothills of the Himalayas, It is a beautiful place, and means so much to me – to us.

Could you both come out do you think? Perhaps mid-February, and Bill and I could show you something of Agra and Delhi before our wedding. Yes – I do mean Bill, (Jim married my flat-mate last Spring), and I would like you to meet him beforehand. He is writing to his parents as well, and it would be wonderful if you were all there to share our happiness . . .'

* * * * * * * *

# THE TOY SHOP

On September 25, 1920 Elizabeth, in brand new school uniform, knee high socks and shiny black shoes, set out for her first day at Bramford High School. Joanna, her elder sister by two years, held her firmly by the hand, especially as they crossed Main Street and turned into Bramford Lane.

Elizabeth paused as they passed Hills' toy-shop on the corner but Joanna said firmly, 'Not now Lizzy, we will stop and look on our way home. I always do.'

They were all new in the 'Preparation' class and were allotted seats according to the register, so Elizabeth Wayne found herself seated by Emma Williams, a charming ginger, freckled, curly-haired, laughing Emma. They took to each other at once and played ball together at break.

Joanna, true to her word, stopped to gaze in the toyshop window on their more leisurely walk home. Hills' was wonderful! Dolls with eyes that shut when lying down, huge dappled rocking horses, wooden red engines that a four-year-old boy could sit in, Teddy-bears, golly-wogs, hoops in every size, spinning tops and dolls' houses with teeny miniature furniture inside and food on the kitchen table. Yes! Hills' was a wonderful shop even if one could only feast one's eyes on its wonderful wares.

The Waynes were not poor! In fact their father, as a journalist, had an excellent salary plus many extras for articles submitted to other newspapers and periodicals. But, with six children (two boys and four girls) to feed, clothe and educate expenses were high and education came highest on the list, and school uniform far more important than new Sunday clothes or expensive toys from Hills.

They were a happy family and their parents made the most of every annual festival. You were made to feel special on your birthday, there were always pancakes on Shrove Tuesday, Hot Cross Buns and coffee for breakfast on Good Friday, swiftly followed by chocolate eggs on Easter Sunday. They played at Bob-apple on Al Hallowe'en and November 5$^{th}$ was celebrated with a bonfire, fireworks, parkin and treacle toffee. Christmas was sheer magic even if Hills' wonderful toys did not come their way. There were always 'Wonderbook' annuals, paints, drawing books, models, dolls tea sets, smaller doll or teddies or skates for the boys, as well as surprises in the stockings that Father Christmas filled. Father also arranged games and competitions with bright new pennies and halfpennies as prizes. They felt they lacked nothing and Hills' Toy Shop was just for gazing at.

As the term wore on Elizabeth and Emma became fast friends and always walked home together, leaving Joanna to walk with her own friends. By then she had discovered that Emma was very rich and only at the High School until she was old enough to go to Cheltenham Ladies College. And Emma never walked home alone. If mama came it would be in the pony trap and she would happily take Elizabeth as well and drop her off in Lauriston Villas, but if Nanny came they walked and could stop and look in the toyshop. One day Emma said quite casually, 'My doll's pram is bigger than that one,' and on another, 'Grandma gave Graham a rocking horse like that one last Christmas.'

They lived at the Manor House, just beyond the little country town, and owned one of the only two cars in the area.

Then the day came when Emma invited Elizabeth to tea, and although she was a little in awe of the rich Mrs Williams, she could not wait to play in the nursery, where apparently Hills' Toy Shop had become a reality. Nanny and Emma called for her, giving Mrs Wayne a promise that they would bring her back promptly at 6.30 pm.

On arrival an excited Emma took her straight up to the nursery and sure enough there were dolls with their eyes closed, sleeping in minute beds with proper bed clothes, the doll's pram, a huge Teddy bear, the beautiful, dappled, shining rocking horse and the dolls' house! Everything a child could wish for!

Elizabeth squatted in front of the dolls' house and asked if she might open it. Emma assented, but before Elizabeth had had time to admire its exquisite contents she said, 'Have you ever seen this?' And with that she produces a circle of string, and putting her hands through it asked Elizabeth if she had ever played 'Cat's Cradles', and before long they were trying to out-do each other with intricate designs. When they tired of that Emma produced pencils and squares of white paper and they each drew a head, and indicating where the neck would be, they folded it down and then drew a body, having exchanged papers, and then ditto for the legs. From that they went on to drawing something and the other guessing what it was, and it seemed in no time Nanny came in with boiled eggs, bread, butter and cake on a tray for tea. The afternoon had gone, oh, so quickly.

At 6.30 pm sharp Elizabeth arrived home and immediately Joanna asked, 'What was the nursery like Lizzy?' 'Honestly, Jo, it was wonderful, it was just like Hills' Toy Shop.' 'And Lizzy, what did you play with?' 'Well, actually, we played with a piece of string!'

\* \* \* \* \* \* \* \*

# THE FINGER MOVED
## or
## A Precis of Daniel Chapter V

The Babylonians were great,
      Belshazzer their great King,
They conquered here, they conquered there,
      And treasures home did bring.

Priceless goods of copper, brass,
      And gold and silver ware:
Robes of linen, silks, brocades
      And crowns with jewels rare.

He reigned in peace, enjoyed his wealth,
      Banquets and feasts he gave
To Lords, their wives and concubines
      (Prince Daniel was his slave).

Prince Daniel saw his temples gold
      At drunken bouts profaned!
Of Yahweh Daniel pleaded,
      But to answer, God refrained.

In drunken brawl and bawdy song
      His Lords, wives, concubine
Were feasting, when upon the wall
      Appeared a fearful sign!

Awestruck, the red and shining face
      Of King, turned ashen white!
A glowing light! A hand they saw
      That moved! An awesome sight!

The finger moved! A script was seen
      By Lords and ladies all,
But in what language? None could read
      That message on the wall.

For seconds, minutes, silence reigned,
      Then pandemonium followed!
What could this mean? This holy writ,
      In this mysterious code!

They called enchanters, wizards too
      And sorcerers, no doubt!
They searched their books and racked their brains
      But none could work it out!

The Queen spoke out, 'In captive here
      You have a Jewish Lord.
He is renowned for telling dreams
      Both here and far abroad!!'

Bring Daniel here,' the King replied,
      If he can tell this hand
In purple robe and chain he'll be
      Third Ruler in this land.'

And Daniel stood before the King,
      (Despised the great reward).
But condescended to reveal
      This writing to his Lord.

'Mene. Your kingdom's days are done,
      Will very shortly end,
And 'Tikal' means that you fall short!
      Too late your ways to mend.'

'Upharsin. Your kingdom soon
      Will be divided through
And shared by Medes and Persians,
      Successors, both, to you.'

Belshazzar sadly died that night
      When Persians took his realm.
And Daniel was the Satrap,
      To Darias, at the helm.


\* \* \* \* \* \* \*

# THE SEA IS CALM TONIGHT

'How much is there exactly then?' Mary Grant removed the tin from the mantelshelf and counted its meagre contents. It did not take more than a second or two, as it was practically empty. 'Seven pence halfpenny,' she answered at length, 'but not to worry, I think we have at least half a pound of flour and a few potatoes, and Daisy is still yielding about half a pint of milk a day! We had bread yesterday and I'll make potato cakes for today. You'd like that wouldn't you, children?' Ten-year-old Jean answered for the three of them. 'Ooh yes, we <u>love</u> potato cakes.'

Dad put his arm across his wife's shoulders saying, 'Mary, I couldn't have a better wife. You never grumble when we cannot put out to sea and there is nothing in the house but . .' As he went over to the window of their tiny croft to see the rain still lashing down, and the swell and rollers of the ocean beyond, as it had been for days, 'perhaps it is easing off a little. When we've eaten I'll go down to the village and see what the others think.' Then he added, 'if it's to be a decent catch we'll have to get well away from the coast so we'll not return till morning.' 'Jim dear,' Mary answered, 'don't take any risks. Seven pence halfpenny will buy us something to eat tomorrow.'

Jim, however, had made up his mind and after the meal he kissed his heavily pregnant wife goodbye, telling her to take good care of herself, and then kissed his three children, dark-haired, blue-eyed Jean and her two brothers, aged seven and four, who were as ginger-haired as himself, and he was gone.

In the early evening, Jean and 'little' Jim walked the half-mile to the cliff edge. The rain had eased somewhat, but the wind was so strong that they hardly made it, and it was really frightening to see the huge waves crashing onto the rocks below. Peering out to sea, Jean thought she could see a tiny black speck on the far horizon. The children raced each other home, carried along by the wind, but later, tucked up in her bunk bed, sleep would not come to Jean as she saw again that tiny black speck in that huge, dreadful, sea and remembered their small harbour in the midst of those jagged rocks.

She had probably dozed off when she suddenly became aware of distress signals far out to sea. Scrambling down from the bunk, she ran to her mother, who was already dressing. 'Mam! Oh Mam,' she cried, 'Will Dad drown?' 'Well, we don't know do we?' answered her mother, trying desperately hard to sound cheerful, 'But I cannot stay here and just wait so I'm going down to the harbour. The other women will be there to watch as well. Now will my Jeanie be her Mam's big girl and look after her little brothers? I should be back by morning, but if I am not, take the money from the tin and take your brothers to school. Buy a small loaf from Mrs Ross on the way, and ask her to cut you each a slice, and I'll see you at the harbour, love, if I'm not home before.' Then Mam was gone too, and poor bereft little Jean was left to look after things. Slowly she went back to bed, where she slept fitfully until morning.

She awakened to a lovely bright, still, March morning. Oh, why hadn't me Dad waited for one more day, she thought. We could have managed on a small loaf for yet another day, even if there'd been only one small slice each. She roused the boys, and while she helped little Peter into his clothes he cried for his Mam! Jeanie tried to feel like Mam's big girl and console him, but was horribly near to tears herself, worrying about Dad and the boat and the distress signals. Why hadn't they come home? She tried to light the stove but the matches were damp and there was no oil to give it a start. Trying hard to sound cheerful, she said, 'Never mind, Mam says I am to take the money from the tin, and we will walk to the harbour to meet her, and if we don't I'm to buy bread and ask Mrs Ross to cut us each a slice, and then we're to go to school and take wee Peter with us. The Dominie won't mind Peter coming for once.'

'But Mam will be at the harbour, won't she Jeanie?' said Peter.

But Mam was not at the harbour, and as they stood on the harbour wall looking out on the still waters, Jean thought again, 'why oh why had they not waited until today?'

Jean tried hard not to mind and trailed her brothers off to the bakery. She purchased the small loaf, asked for three slices to be cut and, trying to sound grown-up and unconcerned, added, with two big tears already rolling down her cheeks, 'Did the 'Princess' come into harbour last night, you see we were supposed to meet our Mam there.' She was going to say, 'What a pity they didn't wait until today,' but by then she was a little girl again and was weeping with worry and responsibility. Kind Mrs Ross, seeing her obvious distress, said, 'So your Mam didn't come home last night, dearie? Not to worry, I'll tell you all I know. Come out to the back here.'

As Mrs Ross spread farm-house butter and home made jam on the three slices and warmed milk at the stove, she told them that she was quite sure that the life-boat had made contact with the 'Princess', but as the Duncraig harbour was so small, and with the wind and sea so rough, they could not risk it among the rocks, so had made for the bigger harbour at Craigapalin, five miles away. Three or four of the women had set out at once for Craigapalin as they had been getting so cold and wet standing about. 'So when you've eaten yer bread, duckie, you go off to school like yer Mam said, and you'll see they'll be waiting for you when you come out at three.' She wrapped up the rest of the bread and put in three small meat pies, and giving tuppence change from her sixpence said, 'And there's something in the packet for yer lunch.'

At 3 pm Mam and Dad were nowhere to be seen and the disconsolate little trio began the mile walk home. Someone told them they had seen Tom McBride with his Missus and once, looking back, they saw Graeme Brown leaving their lane for his croft over the hill. Then they ran the rest of the way to their own croft, thinking that perhaps their parents had not waited for them in the village but gone straight home. They arrived, breathless, only to find the little croft as cold and empty as they had left it.

The boys said they were hungry, but Jean told them to save their bread for the morning because they would be hungry again then. Suddenly she remembered. Daisy! So with Jim holding the cow's head she tried her hand at milking, but Daisy would not co-operate and she only managed about three tablespoonfuls. This she fairly divided between two saucers, hopefully shook out the last few grains from the bottom of the sugar tin, cut a slice of bread in half and broke it into the two saucers of milk, thinking, well at least it's something for them, and there was still half a loaf for the morning! Later she suggested a walk to the cliffs to occupy them and perhaps help them to sleep better. Well, before sunset they turned for home with poor Jean thinking of a whole night with two hungry boys, when round the bend of the lane she saw the Doctor's gig approaching. Someone was ill! Where was he going? Suddenly, he turned his horse into their own little path to the croft. Dragging Peter, they raced the last fifty yards home, arriving just as the gig drew up. 'Here we are then,' said the big jovial doctor cheerfully, and pushing a warm bundle into Jean's outstretched arms said, 'You hold that Lassie while I help your mother to her bed. She's had a very hard day and must rest for a day or two!' Jean looked down at the tiny bundle in her arms, and two blue eyes in a very pink face opened for a minute, and a tiny hand stretched its minute fingers.

Jean looked up at her Dad with big questioning eyes as he unpacked the shopping. 'It was a wonderful catch, lassie,' he said, 'but we developed engine trouble and a sail would have been ripped to pieces, let alone the risk of running onto the rocks. Nor could we risk the little harbour so we made for Craigapalin. It's a good market there and more money, but your Mam shouldn't have taken that five-mile walk, for suddenly she told us that 'little Mary there' was on her way into the world! Mrs Brown took her to the local clinic whilst I finished the selling and shopping. We wondered how we were to get home but the good Doctor there said he would run us home when he had finished his clinic. Now, come on, lassie, you and I must get busy with a rabbit stew, and there's a sugar stick for each of you afterwards! The sea is calm tonight and our engine repaired, so we are off again after supper whilst the fishing is excellent and the market good!'

Two hours later, as he kissed them all goodbye, he whispered to Jean, 'And you'll be yer Dad's big lassie and look after yer Mam and don't let the boys trouble her.' Jean saw the boys into their bunk and then, with a comfortably full tummy, climbed into the big bed with her Mam, and with wee Mary between them. She fell into a long, contented, dreamless sleep.

\* \* \* \* \* \* \* \*

\* \* \*

### 'FIREWORKS'?

*Three-year-old Nicky lived in a modern, centrally-heated semi-detached house in the south. In early autumn he visited his Grannie in the north, where a coal fire was lighted in the sitting-room each evening. Nothing was said regarding this phenomenon, but on his return to the south Nicky was heard describing it to his neighbour's child. 'My Grannie,' he said, 'has a bonfire in her lounge!! She burns dirty stones on it!!'*

\* \* \* \*

# A LONG, LONG TRAIL AWINDING . . .

There had been nothing wrong with family life and in a way they quite enjoyed the neighbourhood and friends with whom they had so long been acquainted. Nevertheless, Sammy fidgeted for change and as the wanderlust took firm hold of him he confided in Celia, and they planned to seek wider horizons together starting that very night.

At dusk they made as big a meal as was possible and then slithered out into the night on a voyage of discovery.

At first the going was easy over stretches of luscious green grass that seemed interminable, but after an hour or so the grass stopped abruptly and they found themselves in an area of scree with a sheer mountain rising beyond it. They tried going along with it but it was horrid and caused them to wobble or slip sideways, so they faced the alternative of ascending the cliff face. Their progress now in 'getting away from it all' and exploring exciting new worlds, was very slow, but they soldiered on. By bearing slightly to the right, as they climbed upwards, it made it easier to cling to the rough surface, but nevertheless it seemed never-ending!

Sammy, at one point, suggested turning back, but Celia insisted that they must reach the top eventually so they struggled on! Up and along and up again and just as the short summer night was beginning to show signs of the coming day, they reached a ledge. It was very difficult to negotiate but somehow they managed to get up and over it, and while comfortably resting there they were able to look back on the long silver trail that marked their progress, and now the way to the very top was of a much gentler slope and would present no difficulties.

The sky was now bright in the east and birds were beginning to sing! Thrushes, blackbirds, all manner of tits, linnets and finches. Hungry birds perhaps! As Sammy and Celia happily surveyed their progress two large, yellow claws landed on the ledge between them, a large yellow beak opened and snapped shut, and as Sammy Snail recovered from the shock of interruption he found that bird and Celia had vanished!

He looked around and realised there was a whole row of mountains with sheer faces and gentle slopes to the apex and each had a stretch of luscious grass leading up to it. He looked again at the two silver trails winding up to the ledge. If he ventured down he might fall. Better to wait where he was and perhaps another nice friendly bird would come along and carry him off to where Celia had gone. The sun was getting warm now so he snuggled into the little house he always carried with him to await the Advent of Celia's blackbird!

* * * * * * * *

# FOOTPRINTS IN THE SNOW

It wasn't so bad in the office as it was air-conditioned, but coming into the street at 5 pm Jerry felt as if he had been hit by the blast of a furnace!! He put his finger round the inside of his collar band. It felt tight and hot. He surreptitiously removed his tie, rolled it up, and as he put it in his pocket was thankful that his flat was only a quarter of a mile away. But not to worry! Delhi might be 119 degrees in the shade, but in a day or two he would be in the Kashmir valley enjoying the cool of the Himalayan foothills. He must call on his friends this evening and tell them his permit was through, well in time for the 26$^{th}$.

At 8 pm he descended from the heights of his fourth floor balcony flat to call on his friends two blocks away. As they sipped cold beer on the veranda, Jerry told the joyful news that his permit had come through so could travel with them on the 26$^{th}$. 'Sorry old chap,' replied Dennis, 'I must have mislead you. We only said the 26$^{th}$ to make sure we had the permits in time but we cannot start out until May 1$^{st}$ as we do not finish until the 30$^{th}$.'

Jerry, however, was not put off but decided to visit Amritza and the Golden Temple en route, and then if he arrived a day or two in advance of his friend what did it matter?! He would happily relax in the cool of the hills for a day or two.

All went according to plan and on the evening of the 29$^{th}$ he arrived in Shrinagar, put up for the night in a tourist hotel, and on the following morning called at 'The Rose Agency' about their arrangements to camp in Palgam. 'Yes Sahib. All ready Sahib!' he was told, 'But very cold in hills this year Sahib. Better you wait here for your friends!' Jerry considered it. They had planned to camp in the hills for three weeks and then have a week on a houseboat on Dhal Lake for the last. After much thought he decided to stick to the original plan as, after all, he had come to the hills to cool off and find his energy again. They argued, but Jerry, being determined, shortly found himself on a bus bound for the hills surrounding the town, hoping he would find everything as planned and with a cook-cum-servant to wait on him.

The representative from the agency met him at the bus stop and escorted him to a most picturesque small plateau, surrounded by pine trees, and beyond them snow covered hills. A light covering of snow also covered the ground and heavy grey clouds blocked out the hills here and there. Two large sleeping tents, and a smaller one for the cook, had been erected just clear of the trees on the western side, and at the furthest end, at a distance of some two hundred yards, a much larger camp had been set up, but as yet obviously deserted. All the way the representative talked. 'Your cook, Kashmiri! He likes cold! This year too much cold, Sahib. Today more snow! Other Sahibs, they stay Shrinagar. Tent alright. Warm, dry. Tonight Sahib perhaps more snow! Other years, April, May all warm, all sunshine, Sahib. This year cold, very cold; better you wait Shrinagar, Sahib.'

Certainly, Jerry was much colder than he ever thought he could be in India. 119 degrees in Delhi and in Shrinagar only 28 degrees. However, the tent was roomy and furnished with two beds, an old fashioned wardrobe and dressing table with drawers (which European home, had they graced in the day of the Raj), two chairs and a table, and through an opening at the back into what seemed like half a bell tent, was a rudimentary bathroom! What more could he wish for?! The cook provided an excellent evening meal and with it brought him a 'kangari', a little earthenware fire basket of glowing charcoals, which he held under the blanket he had draped round his person for extra warmth. He read by the light of a lantern until 9 pm and then decided he would be warmer in bed.

Sleeping in a tent at a temperature below freezing was no joke. The mattress seemed so thin. He doubled his blanket over his sleeping bag, but still he was cold. He added his dressing gown and his light overcoat and sleeping fitfully the night crept on. Midnight! One o'clock! The silence seemed oppressive. Where was the servant? Possibly gossiping with the servant at that other camp.

Did he hear a sound? Was it footsteps? There <u>were</u> sounds. Someone was pulling at a guy rope. A body fell against the tent wall! His hair was standing on end, he was petrified with fear. Now heavy footsteps encircled the tent. It must be mountain thieves come to kidnap him. He was terrified. They were pulling on the guy ropes on the other side now. They were going to force an entry from both sides at once. Should he dress quickly? He was too frightened to move. More heavy footsteps that slowly died away. Did they think the tent was uninhabited? Would they return? He lay awake for hours, it seemed, but sleep came at last.

A hand touched his shoulder and he screamed aloud, but as he opened his eyes he saw only the friendly face of Byjam, his servant. 'Bed-tea,' he said; 'Sahib very tired and not waking up.' He opened up the flaps of the tent, saying, 'See Sahib today sunshine and soon snow will go! Sahib get up now and come and see. Last night big, big Aswal coming. See! See!' Jerry, still tired, reluctantly got to his feet and put on his shoes and dressing gown. He followed Byjam out of doors, expecting to see the footprints of marauders, but there clearly in the snow were the footprints of some large animal that had obviously circled his tent, tripped on guy ropes and indicated the way by which he had come and gone through the trees to the rising ground beyond. Aswal? A brown bear, and by the size of those footprints he must have been a pretty big one.

Oh well! Only one more night and then his friends would be joining him.

By then his panic of the night would have abated and the experience would make good telling at some future date!

\* \* \* \* \* \* \*

# THE STRANGER ON THE TRAIN

'Here, lass, let me do that!' And before she could murmur independently that she could manage the large, heavy, cheap, cardboard suitcase, that contained all her worldly goods, it had been lifted from her grasp and placed on the rack above her corner seat in the empty railway carriage. He flung up his own luggage, a kind of kitbag and a much-labelled, battered, leather suitcase, on to the rack, travel brochures on to the seat opposite, and then disappeared in search of liquid refreshment.

The day was hot and Euston Station exhausting, the atmosphere thick with noisy engines letting off steam, the smell of smoke and coal-dust and pushing sweating crowds. Poor Agnes had hardly ever travelled and certainly not alone before, but nevertheless in spite of the bustle she had found the right platform, the right train at the right time, and she now straightened her battered straw hat, wiped the perspiration from her face and waited for the train to start. The man who had helped her with her luggage took his seat as the train moved from the platform.

Before very long she was looking out at the passing fields, trees, villages and factories, as the great locomotive steamed northward, and her slightly worrying adventure had begun.

Agnes was eighteen and apparently alone in the world. Her mother, having married late to an elderly friend, had not anticipated a family and both were pleasantly surprised when at forty-three she had given birth to Agnes. When the child was five-years-old, because of the depression in the north, they had come south to East London, and before she was nine her father had died.

Fortunately her mother had been thrifty and careful. She had worked long hours as a machinist in a factory and had managed to pay the rent of five shillings a week for their four-roomed terraced house, a penny a week each for sick benefit and the same for insurance for funeral expenses.

At fourteen Agnes had left school and had started an apprenticeship at a large departmental store, earning five shillings a week for the first year and seven shillings and sixpence for the second. They could have managed comfortably but mother fell ill. She struggled to work for a year and Agnes for another two, but in the end had had to give up and stay at home to nurse her mother, who had died in agony of cancer, a year later. (The doctor had said she was a capital nurse, but that did not help as she had stood tearfully at her mother's graveside, wondering what the future held in store for her). Dear mother, she had discovered, had also managed to save fifty-four pounds, six shillings and fourpence in the post office savings bank, and had done so in Agnes' name. At least she was not absolutely destitute.

Agnes had been warned not to talk to strange gentlemen but this young man was so out-going and friendly she found herself sharing something of her recent troubles and uncertain future. He seemed to have no time for conventions and, saying that he had understood that England was always cold, first removed his jacket, then his tie, opened his collar, and finally rolled up his sleeves, revealing strong brown arms. Presently he added, 'And where are you off to, lass? A nice holiday somewhere?'

'Well,' answered Agnes, 'I don't really know, I have a little money, which I hope will keep me until I find my aunt or cousins perhaps.'

'But haven't you an address to go to?'

'Well, no! Not yet! I am going to Penrith and then on to Mardale. I shall go to the rector there and I am hoping he will know of a bed and breakfast for me whilst he looks up his registers for, perhaps, someone who belongs to me. You see, it's where my parents came from.

'You and I,' he drawled, are a pair of wanderers. I landed at Tilbury two days ago from Sydney in Australia, after six weeks at sea, and as soon as I was through customs I took a train to Liverpool

Street Station. I left my baggage there and bought a guidebook, and then I walked to St Paul's, Marble Arch, Hyde Park and Piccadilly Circus, and all the places I had heard about. I walked on the Embankment, The Strand, Fleet Street, and all the places my ole Granfer had told me about. I slept in the station waiting room and ate in the buffet, and now I am on my way to Dumfries to see my Granfer's sister-in-law. He has kept in touch fairly regularly, at least my Gran did until she died, and Granfer carried on. Haven't you got any Aunts or Uncles?'

He was perhaps ten or twelve years older than she was and yet so settled in what he was dong and so self-assured that he seemed older. How she envied him setting out to visit a real person, even if he had never seen her before, rather than a hypothetical one.

'Now tell me. Who have you in mind to visit first, and where will you go tomorrow?'

'It is so difficult to explain,' she said. 'I seem to be in the wrong generation. My mother was the youngest of three and a bit behind the other two, and her brother, the eldest, went to Australia and I am hoping to find my aunt, who shouldn't be more than seven or eight years older than my mother, who was more than forty when I was born. My father died when I was nine and my mother three months ago. My mother often spoke of her elder brother and sister, but I cannot remember my aunt's surname. She must have married about fifty years ago. I am hoping to find her Christening, and then her wedding. Grandmother's three children,' she added, 'were so spaced out it was like bringing up three only children.'

'Funny,' he said, 'But my grandfer had a little sister, but I know she did not have a stiff name like Amelia.' Can't remember what he called her now.'

The journey passed so pleasantly she began to feel as if the stranger opposite had been a lifelong friend. She even told him how their landlord had put up her rent in order to get her out, and how she had argued with the furniture dealer, who had cleared the house, and that she was travelling on the fifteen pounds he had eventually paid her.

Agnes had had a bottle of water to drink with her sandwiches at midday on the station, but Frank, her fellow traveller, had insisted on buying coffee for two when he ordered his evening meal from the buffet, and when they reached Penrith, at 4 am, he naturally lifted her case down from the rack and put it down on the platform; then suddenly, just before the train carried him on to Carlisle, he pushed a scrap of paper into her hand, saying, 'That's my great-aunts address. Write to me there if you cannot find your aunt at Mardale.' She pushed it into the wooden handled canvas bag at her wrist.

As the train shunted off, on the next leg of its journey to Carlisle, poor Agnes felt almost as bereft as when she had left the cemetery on that cold late March morning.

The sky was already golden in the east when she settled in the waiting room to wait for morning! She dozed, wakened and dozed again until 7 am and then sought out a porter, or the stationmaster. For the princely sum of three-pence she was permitted to leave her case for twenty-four hours, and was about to ask the way to a bus-stand when a notice on the mirror caught her eye. 'GFS Members' it read, 'needing assistance should call on Mrs Bailey at number five Green Street, Penrith. Having been a member she asked the direction, and before long found herself drinking tea with a new found friend and later being taken to the bus for Mardale.

The kind rector was studious and delighted to find a bit of genuine research that needed doing. First they went to the present Baptismal Register, and sure enough her name was there, born May 3rd 1904, and five years before that her parents' wedding had been recorded, but he had not any older registers. He said they must be in the Diocesan Register Office at Carlisle, and if she could tell him all she knew he would try and trace them for her. He, laboriously, wrote it all down and then said, 'you leave it with me, Miss Brownlea, and then come back in three weeks to see what I have discovered.'

He chatted happily all the way back to the bus station, and even suggested writing to the immigration offices in order to trace her uncle, but Agnes was thinking, eight pounds, ten shillings, would that keep her for three weeks? Perhaps Mrs Bailey would know of a cheap bed and breakfast. But on arrival back in Penrith good Mrs Bailey had done more than find her digs. At the biggest shop in town they needed extra staff for two weeks to help with the summer sales, 'and you can go for an interview tomorrow!' How fortunate that you are in mourning,' she added tactlessly and cheerfully, 'for you have to wear a black dress in the store!!' And one more thing she had said was that they board their assistants, so they will only pay you five shillings a week pocket money, and of course you can stay with me tomorrow and until you go on Sunday.

Agnes was both relieved and delighted, especially when she learned that there would be two others starting with her. Again fortune smiled on her when a girl went off sick in the hosiery department so she bravely requested that she might stay on for a third week; and on Thursday, her half day, went off to Mardale to visit the rector, hoping against hope that he had news of her aunt and that she was still living.

He was delighted with the success of his findings. Three generations were not so far back after all!! He told her of her aunt's marriage but felt that Sheffield was too large a place to go searching for someone of a common surname like 'Smith', but he had done much better with her uncle's family. He had married their cousin, Margaret Spence, and she had bravely gone out to Australia, alone, to marry him. Margaret always kept in touch with her sister, who lives in Annondale, a dozen or so miles from Carlisle, and who is longing to meet you as soon as you can arrange it. I wrote to her from Carlisle.

He gave her the slip of paper, on which he had written the address of eighty-one year old Mrs Mary Miller, which she carefully folded up and tucked it into the bag she always carried at her wrist. He chatted happily about how he had traced all the information as he accompanied Agnes to the bus, and then just as it was about to start he said, 'Oh, I nearly forgot! A large young man came here enquiring for you a day or two ago,' but the bus had started before he could say more. A young man? Perhaps the son of the aunt-in-law, she thought.

Thursday to Monday seemed an eternity, but it gave her time to send a postcard to this unknown relative, who possibly knew of her real aunt, and to thank Mrs Bailey for all her kind help.

She found an early train to Carlisle and a bus to Dumfries, which fortunately went through to Dornock, and whilst the conductor retrieved her heavy case from the roof rack, she searched in the canvas bag, at her wrist, .for the slip of paper the rector ha given her. As she read Rose Cottage, Mill Brae, she realised that that was not the rector's writing, and before she could search again she found herself embraced in a bear hug that took her breath away. Released, she looked up into the face of the 'stranger on the train'.

'Frank,' she murmured, 'What are you doing here?' 'I'm staying with my great aunt, who I think is your cousin. I just had to come and meet you! I tried to find you in Mardale, and then had to wait until you had seen the rector again. I have never known such a long week! Aunt Mary knows your aunt's address, and we will go and see her before I go back. When Granfer talked of home he referred to your mother as 'Li'le Milly', which didn't sound a bit like 'Amelia', so I didn't recognise the connection.'

'Mill Brae is only two turnings away, Agnes. I know we have only just met, but when my leave is up I do want to take you to meet Granfer, and then I hope you will let me look after you forever.'

'Frank,' she answered, 'I am at the moment looking forward to meeting my aunt's family, who are of course all strangers to me, and afterwards I shall be so happy to be with you always and to settle among my uncle's people! I know!! Let's get married here with a big family party. Perhaps the old rector at Mardale will officiate, and then we will celebrate in Australia with another family party!'

Lying in bed that night in her second cousin's pretty cottage, she began to work out how far five pounds would go in providing a trousseau, and if there would be some change, as she would like to take 'Granfer' a nice present from England.

\* \* \* \* \* \* \* \*

# DAD'S ORCHID

Dad retired five years ago! At first he was completely lost until he decided to dig over a biggish piece of our garden, just beyond the potting shed, and grow vegetables. He was proud of his efforts, delighted in supplying the kitchen with peas and beans, sharing his tomatoes with our neighbours and plaiting strings of onions to hang up in the potting shed for use in the winter. His carrots and potatoes, in his estimation, grew enormously, as he discussed gardens with his friends in the local village pub.

After a year or so he decided to compete in our annual vegetable and flower show, but Farmer Giles' pumpkin always outstripped all the other entrants, and Tom Handley's gnarled fingers produced such carrots and onions that Dad's looked positively puny. He did once manage a 'highly commended' for his potatoes! Poor Dad! He had tried so hard!

However, undismayed, and without giving up his vegetables, he turned his enthusiasm to our small greenhouse and began nurturing flowers from seeds. Perhaps here he would achieve success among his gardening neighbours. Wallflowers, lupins, delphiniums, all captured his interest, and then all were forsaken in the development of one large, perfect orchid.

He received the seed from a friend. 'Cypripedium Insigne' he was told. He planted it and looked anxiously at the pot each day until the first shoot appeared. He fed it, watered it, watched it, talked to it, almost day and night! It grew strong! But was it growing too tall? Would it outgrow its strength? He put it out by day and under cover at night! Was the greenhouse too warm? Would it do better in the house? The bud appeared! Oh dear, the anxiety! Would it flower in time for the show? More 'Oh dears.' Would the flowers be over before the show? That would be worse! A week to go! The bud showed touches of colour. Not yet. Not yet! Thursday, with just two days before the show it opened in all its glory! Never had there been such a bloom! The soft colours, the almost symmetrical spots, the big pouch, the wing-like petals. Surely this was a prize bloom! Friday came and went and he felt his orchid had reached perfection!

Friday night was so hot sleep would not come! He tossed and turned and looked at the time every half hour or so until at last it was time to get up and take his wonderful Orchid to the village show. The day seemed somewhat gloomy and overcast as he went to the greenhouse to collect it. To his amazement it seemed bigger and better than ever, at least six inches taller! Never had he seen such size, such colour, such splendour! Down the village High Street he went, bearing his precious burden and into the meadow. All seemed strangely deserted, but there was the big marquee ready to receive the entries. With great pride, holding his exhibit aloft, he entered the tent, tripped over a guy rope, rolled over trying to keep his precious orchid from the ground and let out a great yell when he saw it bending from the middle. His pride and joy a ruin!

He tried to sit up and then as he opened his eyes he realised that his wife was gently nudging him awake. 'What is the matter dear?' she asked. 'Did you have a nightmare? Anyway, here is your tea, and don't be too long as today is the day of the show!' She pulled back the curtains and the sun streamed in. It was going to be a lovely day!

Incidentally, Dad's Orchid <u>did</u> win the first prize in its class. The other one came second!!!

\* \* \* \* \* \* \* \*

# THE FAMILY HOME

Was there an infinitesimal pause and a momentary arrested look in his eye before he answered? However, the answer he gave his cousin sounded spontaneous enough; 'Who is the observant little watchman then?' he teased. 'I took it down yesterday to give it a dust when I realised just how dirty it was! I was going to ask you about having it cleaned when I realised I was going to pass Pearce & Co, that do that kind of work, so thought I may as well take it along with me as I went on afternoon duty. I should have mentioned it to you, of course! Incidentally, I am on mornings from tomorrow.'

'You forget I lived here once so cannot help missing things and you have really no need to bother about anything in the house, as I once told you. In fact, Brian and I have decided to more or less move back here now whilst mother is so ill, as I feel I should be on the premises. Her housekeeper and companion are very good, but as her daughter I feel she needs me. The children will also come but Brian says he will see about the sale of our house before he joins us, but will of course be with us at weekends. I shall be in to help Jenny prepare for the influx of the family.'

\* \* \* \*

Mary could never quite bring herself to trust William Brookes, who had turned up on her mother's doorstep from Australia claiming cousinship, and her mother (also Mary as was her mother before her) had, of course, welcomed him in and invited him to stay for as long as he wished! But mother was a sick woman! Chronically ill with diabetes, and gangrene had developed in her right foot. Mary herself felt his credentials should have been more closely examined. How could they possibly know whether he was indeed the great-grandson of her great-aunt Louisa, who had married and afterwards emigrated to Australia when Mary's Grannie, an afterthought in the family, was but six years old.

She had been more concerned than ever when one day he had brought up the question of inheritance. But I understood he had said,

'That my great-grandmother and your grandmother were sisters so surely this house, and all its contents will be divided between their descendants . . .' and Mary had to explain that the large, beautiful house, the treasures it contained, and all the wealth behind it, had only come into her family through her grandmother's marriage to the wealthy Mr West and nothing to do with Louisa at all, except that his very wealthy father, as a wedding present to his daughter-in-law, had paid for Louisa and her husband to come to the wedding and to stay for a holiday. And now this William had removed a small but valuable picture!

As Mary walked home she became more and more worried and wondered what else might have been removed and who William Brookes really was! He certainly knew more about her family in Australia than she knew herself. Louisa had died giving birth to her third child shortly after Mary's grandmother's wedding to the very wealthy Mr Henry West. Grannie had continued to remember the birthdays of her nephews and nieces but they had lost touch after the grandparents and Louisa had died.

Mary had grown up in the big house as her parents had occupied the top floor for some fifteen years before taking over the whole house, and now mother was very seriously ill, although only seventy years old. The gangrene had spread and she had had to have her right leg amputated, and now her left foot was affected. Would she survive a further operation?

On arrival home it was good to find their two children in bed and her husband Brian in his study playing with his new 'toy', his computer and discovering how very versatile the thing was. 'It is amazing what it will find out for you,' he said.

'If it is as clever as all that see if you can discover anything about my great-aunt and her family. She was Louisa Alford before her marriage to Edward Hunter about the turn of the century, or shortly afterwards, and then emigrated. Grannie was about six at the time, as her sister was sixteen years older.' She went on to tell him about the missing picture and that 'pregnant pause' causing her, more than ever, to mistrust William Brookes.

They got really excited as they found together various facts regarding the Hunters but it seemed that there was not one of the name of Brookes among Louisa's children, grandchildren or great-grandchildren. Matilda, Louisa's youngest, born sometime after Mary's grandmother's wedding and her mother's birth, was still single and in the land of the living and aged seventy four! Mary did remember that she once visited England when she was at school.

Having decided that it must be about 9 am in Australia they thought they would try and get her on the telephone, which after many delays and difficulties, and finally much surprise, they managed. Here, too, they drew a blank. Aunt Matilda knew of no William Brookes in their greatly extended family. It left Mary and Brian very puzzled because William had so much family knowledge. Even to the size of her mother's house.

Mary made some coffee and as they sipped it before retiring the phone rang. Brian answered and Mary heard, 'Well fancy! Yes, yes! Well I never! Well, knowing what Mary has just told me about a picture I am sure it <u>must</u> be one and the same!'

When he finally put the phone down he said, 'That was Aunt Matilda again because she remembered that her brother John had a stockman named Brookes, and his son Billie was always playing around with John's youngest. He was third generation Australian but never took to the Australian way of up-country life. 'After my visit to England,' she said, 'He was forever questioning me, I thought enviously, about my aunt's big house in England and how rich she was.' She had then added, 'I never thought of him as William Brookes and we lost touch with him after he became an antiques dealer somewhere in Melbourne. We did hear that he and his partner had been in trouble over some slightly shady business or other and that since then they had started up again in a suburb of Sydney and is doing very well.' 'I felt,' said Mary, 'that there was something fishy about the man, and I had better make sure that mother's valuables are catalogued and fully insured.'

A sleepless night followed, but by morning Mary had come to a decision. Why not move into the big house now without waiting until after they had inherited. Easy enough on the pretext of being near mother whilst she was so incapacitated and seriously ill. She knew Jenny (mother's companion) would be glad to be relieved of the responsibility, and if Maggie wished she could continue as cook/housekeeper to the family, 'and the children love Grannie's big garden!' she added. Alternatively, they could occupy the whole of the top floor as her parents had done when first married.

Brian went to the office and Mary took the children by car to school and then drove on to her mother's. She talked with the housekeeper about the extra provisions that would be needed and a delighted, relieved Jenny offered to help with the beds and to arrange for the opening up of the dining and drawing rooms.

Leading from the library was her father's little safe-room. She found the key, opened up and descended the narrow staircase into the tiny room below. She had expected it to be empty but was not surprised to find that the lock of the door, leading by a devious passage to the main cellar, had been broken. Obviously there was little that the unwanted guest had not explored, and on a shelf was a large, fairly strong cardboard carton. Opening it up she found it contained number s of small articles, well wrapped up in newspaper, and on the top was the small original 'Constable', the latest addition to William Brookes collection from their home.

Naturally many of their valuables were in safe custody at the bank, but on opening the packets she found small items of china, ornaments and jewellery that had been in her grandfather's family for perhaps as long as two hundred years. She wondered whether William intended selling them or making cheap copies to sell, at exorbitant prices, as genuine antiques.

Mary, knowing that Maggie and Jennie were fully occupied, fetched an old suitcase from an attic into which she put the contents of the carton. Then arming herself with a dozen or so old newspapers and a stack of smallish irregular pieces of wood from a small tree, recently chopped down, and a few pieces of rock for weight, she soon had another pile of small parcels with which she refilled the carton, carefully putting the small picture on the top as she had found it, and hoped that the deception would not be noticed.

Then, feeling more relaxed, she enjoyed a cup of coffee with Jenny and her mother, who was delighted to hear that the family were to move in with her at once, then drove Maggie to the Supermarket to do the extra shopping before taking the case home out of the way.

William came in around 2 pm, having lunched at the canteen at the bus station where he had found a temporary job! Mary told him of her plan to bring the children and live with her mother at least until after her next operation. 'In fact,' she added, 'I am bringing them straight from school today, and once we have made decisions about bedrooms, etc., I will be bringing a few more of our things over. Brian will only come for weekends until we have sold up.'

Did she again see that momentary arrested look before he answered, 'Great! It will be an opportunity to really get to know you before I return to Australia.' Then he added, 'whilst you are out I will pop round to the shop and get that picture back! I expect it will be ready!'

Three days later William spent a day in town, and two days after that said he felt he had overstayed his welcome and had arranged to travel by land-rover, with a friend, as far as Ceylon, and then by cargo boat to Darwin, and again overland for the rest of the journey!

Three days later found Mary and Brian helping him to pack his goods into the land rover. Mary, herself, lifted the precious carton (now well tied up) for the would-be thief on his journey.

They waved them off with all sorts of messages for their relatives, especially Aunt Matilda, but, sadly, none of the family ever heard from him again!

\* \* \* \* \* \* \* \*

\* \* \* \*

## '*O LORD TO US THE GRACE DO GIVE US, TO SEE OURSELVES AS OTHERS SEE US!*'

*Eight-year-old Giovana came from Australia on a visit to Grannie's sisters in England. At tea, in the garden, she met first Auntie Dorothy, then Auntie Florence, then Auntie Winnie, etc., etc., for the first time. She realised at once that these Aunties were nothing like Mummy's glamorous sister, her real Aunt, in Australia. Presently, groping for a word that would explain the generation gap, she looked round at the aged, white-haired bevy of fading beauties and asked: 'Grannie, did you say these are 'second-hand' Aunties?!'*

\* \* \* \*

# THE TREES ARE IN LEAF AGAIN

'A new day,' thought Mrs Olive Lodge, as she took her late husband's stout ash-plant from the stand and opened the front door of her tiny cottage, but walk she must, as she saved the heating that way.

They had managed so comfortably before Will had been snatched from her during a particularly hard winter three years ago. In those days he had grown vegetables, enough to serve them all through the winter, and most important, they had always managed to fill up their coal bin during the long warm days of summer, which had helped considerably through the long, dark, cold months of the winter.

She still grew spinach, which went on until Christmas nearly, and a few root vegetables during the summer, but the coal reserve was very small, or non-existent. However, she must not grumble; she had one and ninepence ready to buy a hundred weight next time the man called and the Church had given her a bag at Christmas.

Life was a struggle, but Olive was determined not to give up her cottage and go on the 'parish'. After all, ten shillings was ten shillings, and she always put the four shillings by for the rent on Mondays before anything else. Only the winters were hard when you had reached seventy-seven years.

She re-arranged her scarf to bring it up to her ears and pulled her hat down a little farther. There was a strong wind blowing from the northeast, straight from the snowy Arctic, she thought, but better than the snow itself.

Now she had reached the common and, walking on the soft grass, felt it was easier on the shoe leather, and to use up more time she would go beyond the pond and then round to the further path for her return journey. How long would it take? One and a half hours? Oh dear? If only the wind was not quite so strong and her gloves thicker. They were wearing thin and hardly concealed her arthritic finger joints, but perhaps next week she would be able to afford fourpence three farthings for an ounce of wool at Mrs Groves', and if she made them large enough she could wear them over her present ones on her winter walks.

She had reached her turning point, and looking up realised that the clouds were breaking, and in the not too far distance the sky was blue in patches and she was no longer facing the wind. Should the sun come out she could probably delay lighting up until well after six o'clock.

Olive's life held few luxuries and she was obliged to practise the strictest economies. A pint of paraffin oil a week was sufficient for her little 'Beartrice' stove for making her morning cup of tea and warming her plate of stew every lunch time. Should there be any oil over she would be able to light her oil lamp on Sunday evening. She always kept four spare candles in the house! At teatime she would light her fire, keep a kettle boiling on the trivet for her tea, and later to fill her stone hot water bottle, before retiring. This latter would keep warm all night and was still warm enough for her ablutions in the morning.

Saturdays and Sundays were her favourite days in the winter as she kept the fire going all day on Saturday and cooked her meat and vegetable stew over it, enough to last her for her midday meal for the whole week, and on Sundays, her rest day, she would light her fire as soon as she came from Church, and simply enjoy its warmth and luxury.

After twenty minutes or so Olive turned to the southwest, and now she was on her homeward path. This led through patches of broom, gorse and heather. Here and there were scanty wind-swept trees of hawthorn and silver birch. The wind was now at her back, or was it dying down? And now the spring sunshine broke through, warming her face! She passed an inviting looking bench but felt it was too early for sitting out. She might take cold.

On she plodded over the soft springy turf noticing as she went that the buds on the hawthorn were getting very fat and the catkins lengthening. Suddenly a brighter green caught her eye, and turning she saw where tiny leaves had burst the calyxes that had held them fast for so long, and were stretching themselves in the sunlight as a newborn infant stretches tiny fingers.

She had to stop and feast her eyes on the sight. March? Marching into April. Spring really was just round the corner and the sun pleasantly warm on her face. Another inviting bench, facing the sun and backed by thick furze bushes, was really too tempting. Perhaps it was warm enough to sit for just a few minutes? She lifted her chin as she felt the sun's warmth, her rigid body relaxed, her hands felt warmer and her spirits uplifted.

There may still be blizzards to come but at least she had had today with the promise that the worst of the winter was coming to an end and the pleasant warm days of spring and summer not too far away.

Ten minutes later she again picked up the sturdy ash plant, and with her heart glowing and a spring in her step, she walked the rest of the way home, to put a match to her fire and then sit and enjoy the best cup of tea of the day.

* * * * * * *

# THE CHIMES AT MIDNIGHT

Raped by her employer's son, turned off with her precious resulting bundle, a mere ten shillings in her pocket, (her month's wages) the little servant girl traipsed towards a village near Eastbourne! This was her third day on the road and she was very tired. She had slept rough, not daring to ask for lodgings because of the baby, and she needed her few shillings for bread and milk! She had not very far to go now but how would her poor, hard-working, honest, moral parents receive her now that she had not only lost her job, possibly her character, and was bringing home a child. Another mouth to feed. It had been a good job and she, too, was a hard worker. She might have risen to parlour maid in time.

She was passing a little Church and wearily decided to rest awhile on the bench inside the porch. From within came the sound of children singing, so she took courage, crept inside and seated herself in the shadows at the back to listen. Inside it was decorated with holly, a tall Christmas tree sparkled at the altar, the atmosphere was warm, and the children were singing carols round the crib. She wept softly, remembering that it was now Christmas Eve and the road cold and dark, and her village still eight long miles away.

Three days earlier at the Manor House, Sir William and his Lady had received the dreadful news that their soldier son had been killed in Battle. This Christmas there could be no celebrations, no joy, as they grieved for their eighteen-year-old boy, their only son, who had been so mad keen to join the army.

At 11.30 pm the Church bell rang calling all to worship, to greet the Christ Child and to celebrate his birth with carols, Communion, and great joy! The Service proceeded, and at midnight the chimes rang out to pronounce to the world that the Christ Child was born. The Rector, Servers, Candle-boys and Choir all processed to the corner, where the Nativity Scene had been set up for the 'Blessing of the Crib'. As the candles lit up the manger there was a stirring in the straw, a little whimper, two tiny hands were raised, and the Rector peered down into the face of a living baby! At first there was a great silence before he was heard to murmur, 'It is a miracle!' Sir William and his Lady left their family pew and came to wonder! Lady Kathryn knelt by the crib and as she stroked the tiny cheek, with one kid-gloved finger, said: 'He is indeed God-sent to comfort us in our very sad loss! We will be happy to give him a home and bring him up, as our own.'

\* \* \* \* \* \* \* \*

*Note:    Legend or True? Certainly the story is a figment of my imagination but it is based on a story of a village in East Sussex, where the Lord and Lady of the Manor House adopted a baby found in the manger of the Nativity Scene one Christmas Eve, and he became their heir. His father, of course, was of the Gentry. His mother occasionally crept secretly into the manor grounds to see him at play, and officially met him when he was about fourteen.*

*GES*

# THE WHITE GARDENIA

Miss Nelson had inherited a thousand pounds from her father plus a small annuity, and rather than become the universal aunt and general dogs-body to the off-spring of her married brothers and sisters she decided to go into a business of her own creating. All the family decried it People of <u>their</u> class did not go into business, but Miss Nelson remained adamant and independent.

She bought, on a very small mortgage, a tall town house in a select square in Bloomsbury. She retained a bedroom and small sitting room for her own use, converted each of three large bedrooms into four curtained cubicles, each with a bed, a corner wardrobe, a set of drawers and a washstand. The large sitting room was on the ground floor, the three attics became sports room and bedrooms for three staff, and in the basement was a large dining room and kitchen.

When all was ready Miss Nelson advertised in 'The Lady', accommodation for young professional people working in London.

The plan worked well and Miss Nelson's cubicles were always occupied. She much enjoyed gracing the dining room with her presence at breakfast and dinner and her residents were always allowed to make themselves a nightcap or fill a hot water bottle in the kitchen before retiring. She was very happy indeed presiding over her chosen family, as well as accumulating a little bank balance for her old age.

1937 was to be the Coronation year of King George 6th and the whole of London was talking of lights and decorations, worthy of this great event! What could she do to co-operate? In Bloomsbury?

At breakfast one day she discussed the matter with her residents. The large sash windows that faced the centre garden (two each on the ground and first floors) had window boxes. Perhaps these could be plated with red, white and blue flowers? Too late for forget-me-nots but cornflowers could be encouraged to flower early, and red geraniums would make a lovely show! The white ones?

Marguerites would be too tall! Would daisies or alyssum show up enough? Then shy little Marilyn, whose father owned a nursery in Kent, tentatively put in, 'Daddy has been trying to perfect a white gardenia and I am sure there will be bedding plants ready by the middle of May.' What joy! What co-operation! Miss Nelson beamed on her residents. Marilyn happily went home at the given time and returned with the plants.

Everything went according to plan! The geraniums bloomed first with a blaze of red, and shortly afterwards a riot of cornflowers, but no white to separate them. Then at last buds appeared on the gardenias. Would they open in time? Only three days to go! Miss Nelson watched them anxiously. Her family returning each evening would hopefully look along the boxes before entering.

On the day of the Coronation Miss Nelson came down to preside over the breakfast table and just had to laugh as the cornflakes were being handed round.

Yes! The first flower had broken its bud! It was PINK!!!

\* \* \* \* \* \* \*

# THE SPANISH FAN

It was her first real Ball! Well! Hardly that! Perhaps we should say her first grown up party in order to celebrate her seventeenth birthday. She had seen it all before, (by leaning over the banisters) as guests had arrived to celebrate the birthdays of her two elder sisters, now both safely married.

It would be dinner at eight for twenty four guests and relatives and then the ball was due to begin at ten, when she would stand with her parents and receive a further sixty guests.

Huntley was not large, as Manor Houses go, but did boast a sizeable drawing room, a dining room, that would comfortably seat thirty, a breakfast parlour, and a variety of smaller saloons, but its pride and joy was the ballroom. This was on the west side of the house, it had three long windows that opened up on to a terrace and it was large enough for at least fifty couples to stand up. Apart from the nursery wing (recently vacated by her youngest brother) there were fourteen other bedrooms, plus those higher up that were occupied by the servants. But the best part of the house, according to the now growing up family, were the attics and lofts where the junk and keepsakes of nearly three hundred years seemed to be stored. The original house had been built in the seventeenth century, but had been improved and added to over the years.

Annabella had loved foraging in the attics, and was often seen on a wet day sitting in a dormer window and puzzling over a bit of paper that she may have found in a derelict trunk.

One find she loved and treasured. It was wrapped in old paper and rags and loosely hidden behind the inner part of a chimneystack and, with it. a letter. Had it been written in English or French she could have read it, or even Italian she might have recognised, but this she could not read, and in any case her whole interest had been in the little parcel which, when opened, revealed a rather gaudy fan. She loved it, showed it to no one and kept it hidden in her bedroom.

Her dress, made especially for tonight, was of white Indian muslin over a white satin under-dress. It was high waisted with a powder blue ribbon sash and had a border of tiny acorns worked in silver. Her indifferent brown locks had been brushed until they shone and were enhanced with a plain silver band. Her only jewellery was a single string of real pearls, the birthday gift from her parents. She had come down to the drawing room looking quite angelic until her mother saw she was clutching the gaudy fan that she had found in the attic, which Annabella declared made her feel really grown up. 'Yes, said her mother, 'like any of the old dowagers of our acquaintance! You must go and change it for the little white and silver reticule I gave you.' Reluctantly Annabella did as she was told.

Now, however, because she liked it she was clutching it again, hardly concealed behind her reticule, as she curtsied to the adults and fondly embraced her friends as they arrived for the dancing.

Did anyone notice how she scanned the groups of newcomers as they arrived? 'Would he? Would he not come?' Her father was plain Mr de Vere, but he owned the Manor House that had been the main seat of the family for years, but the one she looked for was the Honourable Carlo de Vere, whose grandfather had sold out to his younger brother, two generations previously. Annabella had seen little of Carlo since he entered Harrow at thirteen, but now he was up at Oxford with her brother, and being on holiday had promised to come tonight.

Then the butlers voice again! 'Mr William de Vere and Honourable Mr Carlo de Vere,' and there they were! Both tall, very dark and handsome, and Carlo nurturing infant side-whiskers into being. Both embraced her fondly in brotherly fashion, kissing her on both cheeks, and then Carlo, holding her a little away from himself, saying, 'Surely this lovely lady cannot possibly be the grubby little Bella who would dare anything and climb as well as any boy could!' I shall insist on leading her into the first dance and taking her down to supper.

It was a warm summer evening and the French windows were open on to the terrace, where refreshments were laid out under pretty coloured lights! Carlo led Annabella to a table and presently returned carrying a tray laden with lemonade, sandwiches and tiny iced cakes, and as he carefully put it down he noticed Annabella toying with the fan. 'Bella,' he said, 'I know that fan! Where did you get it?' He took it from her and opened it on the table! Now he was gazing at it through his quizzing glass and presently said, 'I think it is Spanish, an heirloom, and once belonged to our Spanish great-grandmother. I think in some way it is valuable. When you found it was there any letter or message with it? I tell you what, I'll get Mama to invite you over on a visit whilst I am on holiday, and you must bring it with you and anything else that was with it, and tell me exactly where you found it.'

Three weeks passed before, on a lovely August morning, Annabella and her mother arrived at Leamington Hall in time for a light luncheon and to stay for a long weekend. It was only about twenty miles, but as they had had two false starts before mother could decide that she had all she needed for three days away from home, the day was indeed warming up.

Lunch over, and during the heat of the afternoon the ladies decided on a little siesta, and had the blinds drawn in the sitting room leaving Carlo and Annabella free to admire the family portraits that had been removed from the manor. Sure enough, on an upstairs landing was their Spanish great-grandmamma smiling down on them from her gilt frame. Black hair, done up with combs on top of her head, and draped with a red, gold and black mantilla gold satin full-skirted dress, and in her hand, fully opened, was the fan Carlo had recognised at the party. There was no mistaking that design of red, gold and black dragons. They were as excited as when, as children, they had rowed across crocodile infested lakes, at dusk, escaping from imaginary pirates and so home to cocoa and bed.

They also looked at the family portraits of that day. Carlo's grandfather, aged thirteen, fair and weak-chinned like his father, various great-aunts, and Geoffrey, aged four, black-haired, brown eyes, and already looking as intelligent as his Spanish mother.

From the upper landing they went down to a rustic seat in the rose garden to look at the letters Annabella had found, especially the one wrapped around the fan. The English letters were just great-grandpa's written to his fiancée, and the other three were in a language neither of them could read! Annabella read well in the French tongue and Carlo was doing a classic degree, but they guessed this unknown tongue must, of course, be Spanish.

'Grandpa used to write to his mother in Spanish because he thought it would please her,' said Annabella, 'but he does not see very well now, being in his eighties. Perhaps if I copied the letter in large printing he might be able to translate it for us. Carlo, you get in touch with William and arrange to come over to our place when he is at home, and I will see if Grandpa can help; that is if his valet will let him. He spends most of his time either in bed or in the library now.'

'Good idea,' said Carlo, but let's have another look at the fan. I feel that even there there could be a secret.'

Annabella produced the fan again, and they noticed that the sticks were thick at the end and sort of threaded on a ring. Carlo took it and examined the ring closely, then inserted his thumbnail into a tiny crack, and with a little click the ring opened and the sticks were released. Carlo gently opened the end of one and out slid a little sparkling glass stone! 'Isn't that clever,' said Annabella, and was about to release another but Carlo stopped her, saying, 'No! You'll have to stay the weekend but as soon as you get home see if your Grandfather can translate those letters and then show him the fan! You see I think they are not glass but diamonds.'

A weekend had never seemed so long, but at least she was able to start on her copying, and on Monday evening his valet allowed her to talk with her grandfather in the library. At eighty-four years he was a little vague at times but at last the whole story was put together.

Great-grandpa, Sir Carlo de Vere, had married an intelligent senorita Henrietta, and she had in time presented him with two sons and five daughters. As Carlo (the second) was her firstborn and Geoffrey her last there were eleven years between the brothers.

The old earl wasted his riches on playing cards for high stakes, spirits and at the race courses, and at the age of only fifty-six was killed in a hunting accident, and his son, Sir Carlo the second, took over the management of the estates. The situation was already bad and now steadily worsened. He was, if it was possible, even worse than his father, thinking he could come about by gambling, and would listen to no one. They were mortgaged to the hilt and the farms let on short tenancies, which meant taking all from the soil and putting nothing back.

Poor Henrietta had grown to love the manor house and saw nothing ahead for her eldest son but a debtors' prison. Troubles were mounting. It was then she had written to Geoffrey, her younger son, who at one time had joined the army, sold out in India, and was now amassing wealth trading in the East India Company stationed in Calcutta. Huntley Manor was his childhood home and, like his mother, he loved it, and therefore complied with her wishes. He transferred to the London Office, where he could put in an occasional appearance, and bought out his elder brother, lock, stock and barrel, as the saying goes. Sir Carlo removed to Leamington Hall, one of their much smaller houses, the management of which was undertaken by his eldest son, the Honourable Mr Carlo (3), who was just out of college and who had inherited the intelligence of his mother and grandmother.

But time passes on, and now the two grandchildren of the two brothers had possession of the fan, which had once belonged to their great-grandmother, the once Spanish heiress, who had married their great-grandfather. Now old grandpa Geoffrey was seated in his favourite chair with the mysterious letter in his hand, young Carlo (No 4) sat on the arm of his chair whilst Annabella sat on a stool at his feet. Grouped around were her parents and brother William as Grandpa, falteringly, read:

'I trust this letter will be found, but not until I have passed on! I am writing in the presence of my Solicitor who, being about forty years younger than myself should be able to guarantee its validity for some time yet. These diamonds are a part of my dowry, but realising my husband's and my eldest son's weakness for gambling, I have held them back, hoping that one day they might redeem Huntley Manor, which I love, for the De Vere family, into which I have married. I cannot describe my grief when I saw my son trying to redeem his losses by getting further and further into debt by deeper and deeper gambling! I felt Huntley would soon be lost forever.

Geoffrey was different. He was trading in India, had become very rich and loved his childhood home as I did. I appealed to him to come home and save the manor, which, as you know he did, and was soon settled here with his wife and their three children. He took up some duties with his company's London Office, where his son is now carrying on in his father's footsteps. I was at the Christening of Geoffrey's grandson, William. Meanwhile Carlo (No 3) was quite different from his father and grandfather, and on moving to the smaller house and estate, although only just down from Oxford, took over the management and really treated his father as little more than a pensioner. The Honourable Carlo (No 4) is just one-month-old as I write. Both babies being dark-haired I feel take after me.

I am too tired to write more so will conclude about the diamonds, which you will find in the sticks of the fan. There are twelve, and worth about one thousand pounds each. Two are to go to the finder, and five each to my dear sweet great-grandsons, William Geoffrey de Vere and The Honourable Carlo (No 4) de Vere, to help set them up in life, and I hope to continue a happy and rewarding life at Huntly Manor.'

Signed and in her right mind,

Henrietta (Carlo) de Vere.

And then followed the signature of her appointed solicitor.

The reading came to an end and Carlo looked at Annabella and said, 'Bella, when I have finished at Oxford, do you think it would be a good idea if we bought the Dower House for our home?' She answered, 'Carlo, did you say 'we'?' 'Of course,' he answered, 'but it will be in another couple of years, I suppose, at least that!' 'C-Carlo. Are you proposing?'

He did not answer, and much to the surprise of the assembled company, he took her in his arms, and the kiss, which followed, was far more lover-like than brotherly!

\* \* \* \* \* \* \*

# THE CHRISTMAS PRESENT

Sudam grew up in Katcherwadi. A very small village in the very fertile, two-mile diameter mouth of an extinct volcano! Millions of years ago the whole area had been volcanic, and their village was so high in those hills that outsiders rarely visited them. The whole area was surrounded by a ridge, marking the lip of the volcano, and just in one place a dip showed the track where the bullock carts came and left.

Seven-year-old Sudam had never been further than the lip and was terrified when he saw the everlasting plain that stretched out and out and on and on beyond it. Only he knew that his mother's village was somewhere out there in all that space. He had no ambition to leave the safety of their village but only to grow up and one day work his father's fields.

His mother had been very ill, and although now recovered was still very weak. Her husband, not wishing to lose her, had vowed before the gods that if they granted her healing he would give her whatever she wished. Perhaps a sari with a gold thread through the border or new silver bangles? Whatever? Weeping, she made her request: 'I have lived with you faithfully all these years as a Hindu, but I was brought up as a Christian, let me go just this once to keep the Christmas Festival with my family, and see my mother's village once more.'

Father thought it an excellent plan and wished he had thought of that himself, but retrieved his manhood as head of the family by declaring in the village that he was sending his wife to her mother's village to rest, which she could never do at home, and that he (nobly) would make do with his two unmarried daughters and their aunt in her absence.

It was fourteen miles to Dharkegaon so they set out before daylight in order to be able to rest and feed the bullocks at midday. Sudam, now seven-years-old, was very apprehensive when he thought of those miles and miles of seeming nothingness beyond their boundary, but trusted in the strength of his big father and their strong bullocks!

Mother seemed to have recovered remarkably as soon as they had started out, and as day dawned and the warm bright winter sun came up Sudam began to enjoy the journey. It wasn't just hills, rocks and wasteland! Why! After the few miles they had covered before sunrise they were travelling through fields and saw a little wada like their own, and further on a second one, and about midday they came to a really big village! Sudam had never seen anything like this, only in pictures. There was a metalled road running through it. A big red bus arrived and people alighted and others bought tickets and were carried away. There was a shack which sold delicious sweet tea, and father bought one for his mother, who gave him the last saucerful. Two motors and a jeep passed and then a man on a bicycle, and then a huge lorry stopped. The cyclist and the driver refreshed themselves with tea before going on down that lovely smooth road. There were people everywhere and vendors selling fruit, vegetables and khau as if it were market day. Sudam, fascinated, wandered here and there surveying a world so different from his own.

All too soon, it seemed, the bullocks were rested, fed and watered, the last five miles completed and he was in the arms of the grandmother he had never seen. Then there were new uncles, aunts and cousins, and they were led from one house to another to drink tea.

That wasn't the only excitement. All his young cousins were talking about a play they were to perform on Christmas Eve, the next day. All the children were in it; so whilst mothers prepared the evening meal Sudam was carted down to the BaiSahib's house for a last rehearsal. When he saw that horrid white face and arms he very nearly ran back to his mother, but she seemed so friendly with the other children that, keeping his distance, he decided to stay.

Christmas Eve dawned bright and clear, promising yet another pleasantly warm sunny day. Bamboos and sheets were set up to make a stage with a curtain that pulled. A bangdi-wala came and

BaiSahib bought all the girls a pretty pair of glass bangles of their choice, and then balloons for the boys. In the afternoon they ran races for sweets, but it was in the evening that the real festivities began.

A bell resounded through the community (one piece of iron clonked against another) and all the children went running to the BaiSahib's house, each carrying something from which to drink, where they were seated in a large circle outside. Each was served on a piece of newspaper, with khau jellabies and bananas and then tea to drink. By then it was getting dark and they all crowded into the BaiSahib's house. The little mudroom was decorated with paper chains, coloured tissue paper balls, and evergreens, and at one end was a model of a baby in a feeding trough with parents, and there were shepherds and kings kneeling, and all was lighted up with candles. Sudam stood and stared. It was all so beautiful and so unexpected and, of course, this was what their play was all about.

They managed to find room to sit in rows and sang carols until the candles were half burned. Then came the greatest surprise of all. Round the model were parcels in coloured paper, and the children were each called by name and were given one. How Sudam envied the children who belonged there and were known! But all was not lost. The BaiSahib then asked if <u>every</u> one had one, and Sudam and the two girls stood because visitors were left out. They were told to close their eyes and face the wall, and when they opened them again they, too, found a coloured parcel at their feet. With this the party was over and the children dismissed with instructions not to open their parcels until they reached home.

Sudam had never, never in all his young life, had a parcel before. He carried it home carefully, and sitting with his mother and grandmother opened his treasure. First there was a warm jacket with sleeves made from stuff like a blanket, but soft and warm. Just right for cold winter nights. Then there was a picture, like the model he had just seen, and that mother said she would pin up in her house when they got home; and last of all, the loveliest thing he had ever possessed. It was a tiny heavy tip-up lorry. It was so small but so perfect, and the wheels went round when he ran it across the floor. It was bright yellow! He put some sand in it and tipped it out in little heaps. His new jacket had a pocket and, wrapping his treasure in its red tissue paper, he put it out of sight but where his fingers could still trace its contours.

The years passed. Sudam married at eighteen, and in due course had children of his own. There was a bad famine and the government arranged 'Food for Work' and some communities sat and broke rocks into small stones, whilst others prepared roads thrown out across the area. They were only mud and stones, but it did mean that in the dry season, within fifty yards of their wada, a bus passed in the morning and returned in the evening. One enterprising young man opened a tea shack at the bus stop and the men of the village would gather there to chat when the bus was due.

As Sudam sat with his friends one evening he saw a white woman approaching. It was fifteen or twenty years since he had seen a white woman! Could it be the same? Surely not? All white women look alike! He remembered how friendly she had been and how the children loved her, so taking his courage in both hands he went to meet her, bending and touching her feet, and she greeted him in like manner. He, and his friends, escorted her to the tea-shack and bought her tea but Sudam ran home and presently returned with a little red tissue paper parcel.

Revealing his treasure he asked? 'BaiSahib, do you remember this? Years ago when I was quite a little boy I visited my grandmother at Christmas and you gave it to me. I thought it was so perfect I have kept it safe ever since, wrapped up and put in the box in my house!'

A little second hand Dinky toy, that had been given a lick of yellow paint before being presented, had become a life-long treasured possession of a small boy now grown to manhood.

\* \* \* \* \* \* \* \*

# "THE MOON SITS . . .
# AND SMILES ON THE NIGHT"

Barbara felt completely and utterly relaxed as she pulled the curtains across the window, shutting out the fading sunset after a fine, late-October day. The full moon, she knew, would be rising at the back of the house. One of those wonderful nights that hardly get dark at all. Heavenly!! She collected her supper tray from the kitchen, just cup-a-soup and a sandwich tonight, and put a match to the fire. Such a rare joy not to have to cook dinner, or talk, and the children had settled quickly, and now she looked forward to curling up on the sofa with a book and later a coffee before indulging in an early night.

Jeremy was at an office party. A rather grand affair as it was the engagement party for the boss's daughter. Barbara should have been there as well, but try as she might a baby sitter was unavailable, so she had had to yield to the pressures of being a mother as well as a wife. Tonight they had been little angels and settled by 7 pm, leaving her free to relax and enjoy her night off.

It must have been about 9.30 pm when she was contemplating that cup of coffee and bed when suddenly the telephone rang, jangling and jarring through the silent house. She rushed to remove the receiver before it awakened the children, and an unfamiliar voice asked, 'Is that Mrs Bannister?' 'Yes,' she answered, 'but who are you? And why are you ringing at this time of night?' 'I'm Mrs Dean, and I live a few doors from your mother.' 'Oh dear! Is she alright?' said Barbara, trying not to sound as panic-stricken as she felt. 'Well, that I can't say,' went on the matter of fact voice, 'but there seemed a commotion in the road, and I looked out of the window and definitely saw your mother being taken away in an ambulance! It must have been about an hour ago, but I have only just remembered that your mother once phoned you from here, her not having a telephone, and I jotted down your number! But I expect the hospital has called you by now.' 'No! They haven't. Can you tell me where they might have taken her?' 'Well no, not exactly. Probably Dartford General from here, I should think.'

Dartford, from Frimley! What should she do? Phone her husband? Probably dancing at the Savoy, or was it the Waldorf? Phone Dartford General! Trying to collect her scattered wits she collapsed into a chair in the kitchen, and looking to the window saw the moon riding high and smiling down on her, and she heard herself murmuring: 'All very well for you, but you haven't got my problem!'

She phoned Directory Enquiries for the number of the hospital but drew a blank on enquiring there, but they did tell her that Erith Hospital would have been nearer to Old Bexley than Dartford! 'Why? Why? Why would her mother not have a telephone installed? Always said she did not like them and could not hear what people said. She would insist on it being put in after this. Telephoning Erith also drew a blank, and then she had the bright idea to phone 999! Here they were quite angry and said if she wasn't on fire, or needing an ambulance or the police she should not have called them. However, they then took pity on her and found and gave her the number of the police in Bexley. Help at last! They said they would make enquiries and phoned back after ten minutes, or so, to say that her mother had been taken to St Mary's in Sidcup, was in the intensive care after a suspected heart attack, and she would find the hospital on the A20 at a big round-about from which turnings were also indicated to Chislehurst and Sidcup!

Barbara was desperate. She <u>must</u> get to her mother. Her husband was out and she could not leave the children!

She phoned Jenny but there was no answer! She phoned Mary. Her husband was out and she could not leave the children! She tried Irene. It was past 11 pm now. Her husband answered saying that his wife was in bed suffering from a virus and 'thoughtless of her' to phone at this time of night! What could she do? The phone rang again. She snatched off the receiver to hear Mary's placid voice saying: 'Why don't you wrap the children up in their duvets, I'll warm the beds in the spare room, and just bring them round here for the rest of the night.' A solution at last!

Write a note to her husband. He probably would not be home before two! Get the car out! Then, two-year-old Judy first as she would have to be strapped into her car seat! Then Timothy. He would probably wake up and have to be told where he was going! Put the guard in front of the fire! Lock the door! Lights! Were her hands really shaking?

Off to Mary's half a mile away! Where was Sidcup in relation to Frimley? M3, M25 going east, A20. I think I should turn somewhere near Orpington to get to the A20, 'Oh God, help me to get it right. Help me to be there before it is too late,' she prayed desperately! The M25 seemed endless, but thank heaven for that lovely moon turning night into day, or at least it would be if it weren't for the headlights of other cars. On. On. On. Through Orpington, Chistlehurst, A20. At last the hospital! It was enormous! At least plenty of parking spaces! Find the entrance. 'Could you please direct me to Casualty. Is this right for Casualty? I'm enquiring for Mrs Hanson, who was brought in this evening.' 'Who are you?' 'I'm her daughter. Is she very ill?' 'I know she was taken to Intensive Care, you had better enquire there! The lift is at the end there, keep left when you leave the lift and the department is at the end of that corridor.'

'Mrs Hanson, please. She is my mother and was brought here between seven and eight o'clock, I think. They tell me it was a heart attack.'

'Mrs Hanson?' Ah yes! We <u>did</u> think it was a heart attack, she was so poorly and in such pain, but the doctor now thinks it was only very bad indigestion, so we have put her in Jarvis Ward where we will keep her under observation for a day or two. You <u>may</u> see her as you have come such a long way, but please try to be quiet as sick people are such light sleepers!'

There were six beds in the alcove, and sure enough there was mother, her white hair spread on the pillowslip. She was dozing peacefully, looking pink cheeked and almost smiling.

Barbara almost collapsed into the visitor's chair, and could have wept with relief. The patient's eyes opened, and she smiled on her daughter saying, 'Oh Barbie, you shouldn't have come, it was nothing after all. And how did you know where I was?

Forty minutes later back on the road, driving at a moderate speed, and as she turned to the west that full moon peeped into the car and, smiling at her, whispered, 'well, it wasn't so bad after all, now was it?'

\* \* \* \* \* \* \* \*

# THE LOST FORTUNE

'Great-Aunt, please tell us again about the games you used to play when you were children.'

Great-aunt Erica, at eighty-seven, could remember much more clearly the happenings of that dreadful night eighty-one years ago than what she had got to do next week, especially as their games as children had always been of the happier days they had enjoyed at the old manor house before the terrors of that night when they had been forced to flee.

In her mind she went back to that dreadful evening. 'Why aren't we going to bed?' she had asked. 'See, Thomas is falling asleep and it's nearly dark.' Mother tried to explain about the invading army fighting, looting, killing and burning the houses down, and father had gone to help drive them away. We knew he had not managed it because sometimes we had heard men slashing their way with sticks, swords, and clubs on that dreadful journey, and grandfather had hidden them in caves, and they only walked at night and they ate stale bread and salt meat and drank from streams. When it had seemed quieter they had come to a road and grandfather had bought a donkey to carry their goods and fresh bread to eat, and sometimes they had been allowed to ride in turns. No, she did not know which way they had come except that the sun had been so hot on her back when they had reached the road and until they reached the old farmhouse, which was Mama's old home, and there they had settled. Grandfather died shortly afterwards and father never came home from the wars. Thomas (Erica's brother) had lived to seventy-five, and his son Edward was grandfather to the present family.

But their games? In the woods to the north of the farmhouse, where they now lived, Erica and Thomas had marked out their own manor house. This was the great hall that was used when other Lords and Ladies came to dinner and all the beautiful silver had been used. Pieces of bark were the silver plates and dishes, a large stone the big silver tureen, from which the stewed meats had been served, and half an old wooden spoon was the large silver ladle and pieces of broken earthenware pots had represented the rest of their treasures.

Sometimes they had played at payday! Flat stones found in the river bed and kept in an old piece of sacking were the silver coins which granddad kept in a leather bag, and a heap of sand and grit served as grain for those who were paid in kind, and Thomas would measure it in handfuls into Erica's pinafore.

Sometimes Erica would be a visitor calling at the manor. She would give her pretending horse to a pretending groom and Thomas would bow to her and she would curtsey and he would kiss her hand and lead her to a fallen tree trunk where they would converse. No! They would never forget those happy days of peace and plenty.

'Great Aunt, why didn't you go back after the war was over?' 'Because there was really nothing to go back to. It was burned out and left in ruins and I suppose the army stole everything worth stealing.' 'But, Great Aunt Erica, did you never go back?' 'No, I didn't, but Thomas did. I was my parents' only child so they left all their money and property to Thomas, and when he felt your grandfather old enough to manage things one winter he did go and eventually located the ruins, which he felt had once been his home.' 'When I grow up I shall go and find them and I shall make them new again and live there and be a Lord again, and Albert can have this,' declared nine-year-old Richard.'

The years inevitably came and went and the boys finished school at The Old Abbey and worked for their father, as they grew, so did their desire to find the manor, reclaim their land and lord it over the surrounding countryside, as his forbears had done more than a hundred years ago. Remembering great-aunt Erica's 'pay-day' game he knew they had sheep-shearers, which pointed to livestock, harvesters meant fields and woodcutters pointed to forestry, probably their chief industry, as their surname was 'Forrester'. How far had they travelled in two or three weeks, and how much of that time had they been in hiding? If only he had asked great-grandfather Thomas before he died. Oh well! That was too late now!

Richard, at twenty years old during the lovely days of a mellow October, when the harvest was safely in their flocks sheared and their dues paid, again approached his father, who said, 'True, it's a wonderful idea, but if you spent our lives' savings on this venture where would be should we have a bad year here?' He added, 'But go lad, there is little work to be done at this time of year, just the hedging and ditching, and see what you can find out! Take Henry with you, he is a good, sound, steady lad. And he would probably enjoy it.' In less than a week Richard with Henry, one of the farm hands, set out to discover what they could.

For a week they walked south, and then took a zigzag course to west and southwest, and always towards the distant hills. They called at the parish offices of villages, trying to find maps showing land distribution, and in the churches the names of their forbears among the parish registers, and after a week nearly, in a book that appeared to have been through fire and water they found that in 1441 a daughter named Erica had been born to Albert and Elizabeth Forrester, and two years later, sure enough, Thomas followed. At least they knew they were in the right place to search for the ruins of the old house.

There must be forests because Richard knew their wealth had accumulated through the sale of great oak trees for bigger and bigger ships; there must be water for transportation to the river and so down to the shipyards miles away; fields where grain could be harvested and hills for the grazing of sheep for the wool trade.

They searched all day where the terrain seemed right but with no sign of a ruin, and the weather had changed and looked like approaching rain, so at dusk they gathered wood for a fire and under a good overhanging rock they camped for the night.

Richard awakened first and found the day dry, cloudy but warm. He was stiff, the ground had seemed harder than usual; he went to the nearby stream and washed and returned to arouse Henry. As he looked down on his sleeping form against the rock face of the hills, seeing a spot clear of lichen and grass, he realised he was looking at a flint wall and their shelter an overgrown ceiling! With tears coursing down his cheeks he called, 'Henry! Do wake up, I have just realised we slept at the manor last night! I wondered why the turf was so hard! I'm so glad it rained or we might have passed it by.' Then, looking up at the overhanging ceiling, added, 'And lucky that it did not come down on us.'

They spent the morning searching for inside and outside walls. Not an easy task with so much rubble, now covered with grass and lichen and small saplings, where upper rooms had collapsed, but providing bricks and flints enough to start the rebuilding, Richard said. They certainly found the blackened hearth of the kitchen and were able to discern some of the inner and outer walls. The afternoon found them on the direct route for the fifty-mile walk home, bearing the good tidings of success, which they were anxious to share! Before leaving, they had again visited the Parish Clerk to register their claim and, of course, Richard had to prove that he was indeed the inheritor of the property and title.

They arrived home, with their great news, late in the evening on the third day.

It took Richard the whole of that winter to prove his claim on the two hundred acres of forest land, and four hundred acres of fields and low-lying hills of grass, but perhaps the biggest step of all was to accept half of his father's savings in exchange for renouncing all claim to the farmhouse, fields and livestock, which would now be wholly inherited by his brother, Albert.

Richard was so sure of success that he immediately set about his plans for the future. He negotiated with shipbuilders at the coast for oak and pinewood, with a barge for transport and at first just three woodcutters from the nearby village, and by the first day of spring he had the deeds of his property in his own name and he could begin business whilst they were building. Henry begged to come, too, but Richard knew he would have to be careful with money for the time being so they agreed that for the first two years they would live together in a temporary shack, which they would put up immediately, and in lieu of a year's wages he would build him a house at the same time as the manor, he would be given a fifteen acre field for his own use, two meadows for grazing, two pigs, two cows and a dozen hens. He would have his present wages for the second year and eventually he would earn the recognised wage as Richard's bailiff. He would then be living in his own house and all this they hoped to accomplish in about five years.

The woodcutters started immediately, large trees for the shipbuilding and small stuff for first their shack and the farm buildings. He bought twenty ewes and a ram, three cows and three pigs, already increasing, and a pair of oxen for drawing their borrowed plough to prepare three fields for belated sowing. Just three weeks behind the normal!

Although weary at sunset they would spend the final hour of daylight clearing the manor site or preparing the foundations for Henry's house.

The autumn brought considerable relief as revenue for the wood began to roll in, and they were able to double the number of woodcutters. They were also able to sell off twenty piglets and some of the grain harvest. During the shorter dark days of the winter they were able to concentrate on the building work.

By the fourth year Henry's house was ready, so he married the pretty daughter of one of the woodcutters, who came to the site regularly with cheese and bread for the cutters. Henry suggested that Richard should move in with them, for the time being, and Richard accepted his main meal but felt there was enough of the manor ready, so he would move in there, and Henry could begin his promised work of managing the estate, while Richard could concentrate on the completion of the manor.

The house was growing apace. The great hall reached the roof but a staircase branched at the far end to lead to five or six upper rooms on either side above the lower rooms, (to perhaps house an extended family in the years to come,) would be completed later.

One evening at dusk somewhere between kitchen and family dining room, he was pushing a barrow of flints when one large one fell from the handcart. The sound was different! He picked up the flint and then dropped it again. It sounded hollow. He dropped to his knees and felt round the large flag stone and realised its cement was, in fact, little more than soil and sand. He fetched a knife and released the stone, and with a super-human effort he pushed it aside, revealing a small cellar below. He kindled a lamp and lowered it into the aperture, revealing a dozen rough stone steps, and descending into what must have been a secret cellar there he found the old coffer. The wood was rotting but the iron lining still intact. It was locked but he found the key hidden in an alcove under the steps. With great difficulty he managed to turn it and opened the box.

He could not believe his eyes! There, dulled with the years of darkness, hidden from all prying eyes and invaders, was great aunt Erica's banquet silver. The large silver tureen and ladle, plates and dishes galore, lovely kitchenware in brass and copper, ewers, pans and spoons and there, in the corner, was a leather bag, stiff with age, but heavy with gold and silver coins. Richard could hardly believe his eyes. Aunt Erica's games had never seemed really true, but here was positive proof!

He thought for a day or two and decided he could spend a little more and hasten the completion of the manor and when he received a message from his father, telling him of his sister's marriage after the lambing and spring sowing, he sent an answer by the messenger, suggesting a double wedding, and with this he was writing to Alice's parents asking for their daughter for his bride and proposing that two weeks after the weddings, they would have a big family party, (including all the in-laws), and celebrate the reopening of house and estate.

In due course all went according to plan. Bedrooms were finished and furnished with large beds and feather mattresses, ewers of water stood on wash stands and two girls from the village would carry hot water to his guests each morning, help with the cooking and wait at table; and in the sitting rooms the divans and ottomans they covered with sheep skin rugs. In the great hall were benches surrounding a long table covered with a white linen cloth, and on the great day silver branched candlesticks would illuminate the whole.

Henry left by ox-cart on the second day after the weddings, bearing their goods, chattels and wedding presents, whilst Richard and his bride came two days later on horseback. From a mile away, seeing the glowing house reflecting the setting sun, Alice thought she had never seen anything so beautiful and knew she would be happy there. On arrival a henchman appeared from nowhere, it seemed, to take their horses to a stable whilst Richard, taking her by the hand, led her up the steps to the open front door of her new home. That night, lying together on the feather mattress of their comfortable bed, he told her of his find in the cellar and how his aunt Erica's stories were true and they made plans for their first big house-party in manorial surroundings.

Before long, with the joint labours of Alice and Mary, (Henry's wife) the kitchen was cheerful with all the bright brass and copperware! They worked on the silver with ash and warm water until it was restored to perfection. They brought up bottles of homemade wine, dandelion, cowslip and elder, from Mary's house, they made bread and sweet cakes and puddings from preserved plums and apples, kept in the loft. They killed a pig and two sheep, which were duly boiled, roasted or salted, and by the great day all was ready. A barrel of ale was purchased from the alehouse in the village for the men.

As their guests arrived at the appointed time, Richard was out on the doorstep to bow to the ladies and lead them to his sitting rooms for rest and refreshment. The great feast being arranged for the second day!

None were allowed in the great hall until the evening but there was plenty to see and do as they wandered about the farm and into the forest, and at sunset all was ready and the visitors called to dine. Elizabeth stood, stock still, in the doorway, seeing the light of a hundred candles reflecting their glow in the polished silverware, and gasped, 'So her stories and games were true!!' Albert, father and grandfather, in unison, chorused, 'So you found it! Where could it have been hidden?' And now <u>Sir</u> Richard told how he had unexpectedly come across it.

Never had there been such a celebration! When the meal was over the fiddlers, who had been hired from the village, played until after midnight when the young people were too tired to dance any more, and all sought their couches for the night.

In private conversation with his father on the next day Richard said, 'Father, I think all this silver must stay at the manor where it belongs, but as there are a dozen or more of the candelabra I would like Albert and Elizabeth to have two each as a wedding gift and a memento of last night, but so far I have not told you about the money. Great-granddad's leather bag, from which he paid the work force, was also a fact, and that I also found intact in the coffer. Six years ago, in order to help me with this restoration of house and business, you gave me half of your savings. I would be happy now to give you half of our great-grandfather's savings in case we ever have to face the proverbial 'rainy day'. He fetched the bag and, coin for coin, they shared the contents, to the satisfaction of both son and father. Particularly father, as he knew now that he would be able to leave his second son as comfortable as his firstborn.

\* \* \* \* \* \* \* \*